D1525255

The

Highlander's

English

Maiden

Loved by a Highlander

Book 2

by Debra Chapoton

ISBN: 9798386324698

Imprint: Independently published

Books by Debra Chapoton

The Highlander's Secret Princess
The Highlander's English Maiden
The Highlander's Hidden Castle
The Highlander's Heart of Stone
The Highlander's Forbidden Love

Christian Non-fiction:
Guided Prayer Journal for Women
Crossing the Scriptures
35 Lessons from the Book of Psalms
Prayer Journal and Bible Study
Teens in the Bible
Moms in the Bible
Animals in the Bible
Old Testament Lessons in the Bible
New Testament Lessons in the Bible

Christian Fiction:
Love Contained
Sheltered
The Guardian's Diary
Exodia
Out of Exodia
Spell of the Shadow Dragon
Curse of the Winter Dragon
   Second Chance Teacher Romance series (Christian themes):
      Aaron After School
      Sonia's Secret Someone
      Melanie's Match
      School's Out
      Summer School
      The Spanish Tutor
      A Novel Thing
  Unbridled Hearts series (Christian cowboy romance)
    Tangled in Fate's Reins
    Rodeo Romance
    A Cowboy's Promise
    Heartstrings and Horseshoes
    Kisses at Sundown
    Montana Heaven

Montana Moments
Tamed Heart
Wrangler's Embrace
Moonlight and Spurs
Whispers on the Range
Christmas at the Double Horseshoe Ranch

Young Adult Novels:
A Soul's Kiss
Edge of Escape
Exodia
Out of Exodia
Here Without A Trace
Sheltered
Spell of the Shadow Dragon
Curse of the Winter Dragon
The Girl in the Time Machine
The Guardian's Diary
The Time Bender
The Time Ender
The Time Pacer
The Time Stopper
To Die Upon a Kiss
A Fault of Graves

Children's Books:
The Secret in the Hidden Cave
Mystery's Grave
Bullies and Bears
A Tick in Time
Bigfoot Day, Ninja Night
Nick Bazebahl and Forbidden Tunnels
Nick Bazebahl and the Cartoon Tunnels
Nick Bazebahl and the Fake Witch Tunnels
Nick Bazebahl and the Mining Tunnels
Nick Bazebahl and the Red Tunnels
Nick Bazebahl and the Wormhole Tunnels
Inspirational Bible Verse Coloring Book
ABC Learn to Read Coloring Book
ABC Learn to Read Spanish Coloring Book
Stained Glass Window Coloring Book
Naughty Cat Dotted Grid Notebook
Cute Puppy Graph Paper Notebook
Easy Sudoku for Kids

101 Mandalas Coloring Book
150 Mandalas Coloring Book

Non-Fiction:
Brain Power Puzzles (11 volumes)
Building a Log Home in Under a Year
200 Creative Writing Prompts
400 Creative Writing Prompts
Advanced Creative Writing Prompts
Beyond Creative Writing Prompts
300 Plus Teacher Hacks and Tips
How to Blend Families
How to Help Your Child Succeed in School
How to Teach a Foreign Language

Chapter 1

H ANNAH SAT IN discomfort in the Beldorneys' carriage, beside her only friend on this earth, Eleanor.

The ride to the kirk was bumpy and jarring. Her stomach churned and her muscles kept tensing. Across from them sat Captain Bernard Luxbury whose complete attention was on Eleanor. Hannah didn't mind being ignored by him or by the McKelvey man who'd captured Eleanor's heart. Her own attention, when the carriage made a turn and she could catch a glimpse of all three McKelveys ahead on horseback, stayed focused on the younger McKelveys, Jack and Logan.

The road smoothed somewhat as they came to a low row of bushes lining the last hundred yards to the stone chapel. The kirk was larger than Hannah expected and, from the direction they came, was preceded by uneven rows of headstones. She could see a vicarage behind the kirk, a modest stone hut with a thatched roof and shuttered windows. Quaint.

"What a funny cemetery," the captain said. He'd been commenting on various things along the way—a picturesque loch, a thatched-roof hut,

1

a patch of new heather—trying to draw Eleanor into a conversation, but Hannah answered for her every time. It irritated the captain and both women knew it. Eleanor gave Hannah secret hand squeezes to thank her.

"It does look odd," Hannah said, nudging Eleanor, "not all the rows are straight like at Ingledew."

"Mm-hm." Eleanor had little to say and Hannah knew why. These last weeks were stressful. They left England, encountered highwaymen, fled to a harbor, and boarded a ship where a phony inspector ordered them to change into filthy boys' clothing. She and Eleanor were adept at impersonating lads, having been raised as stablehands, their feminine traits suppressed, but becoming part of the plot to dethrone King George was becoming too much for both women. Eleanor's royal identity was no longer a secret. All this fuss, with wigs and gowns and balls and feasts, was all for Eleanor. However, Hannah wasn't a tad bit envious. Her thoughts were on Logan McKelvey and also his younger brother, Jack, the handsome lad who had introduced himself to her yesterday at her bedroom door, hand to heart, bowing deeply, flashing eyes and dimples and turning her insides to mush, the same as every other McKelvey.

She was silly to spend any time at all dreaming about these wealthy Scotsmen. She hung from the lowest rung of the social order. Hannah Pascoe of Feock, Cornwall, orphaned and sent to live as companion to Eleanor at Ingledew castle. A mere English maiden. Penniless. Considered illiterate. And only recently taught any manners at all.

Now here she was with Eleanor who'd learned but a few weeks ago that she might be a royal heir. A secret, but soon to be acknowledged, princess. The two of them had been sent to Scotland and Hannah had vowed to Eleanor that she would stay at her side whether she decided to embrace all the courtly high society trappings or run away. She bounced in her seat as the coach hit a rut. It stopped behind their hosts' better carriage.

They had to wait as the Beldorneys' coach let out its five occupants, including a McKelvey sister, Fenella. At last, their carriage moved closer to the door. The horses' hooves scraped on smooth stones, and the carriage stopped. Luxbury stepped out first and held a hand up for Eleanor to grab. She ignored him, keeping both hands on her skirt to lift the hem. She stepped down unaided and Hannah followed. There was no helping hand from the captain for her only a rather loud snort of amusement from one of the McKelveys. Hannah's eyes darted to the three brothers and her heart skipped a beat. She could never choose one over the other; each man was breathtakingly handsome, so alike with dark wavy hair, broad shoulders, well-muscled arms, and sparkling eyes. There was mischief in Jack's eyes, curiosity in Logan's, and adoration in Keir's. *Ah, but that's not for me. Keir only has eyes for Eleanor.*

She startled out of her spell as Eleanor took her arm and quickly pushed passed Captain Luxbury. Hannah stared at the church, its grey stones exactly matching the sky on this cloudy morning. The air hinted of impending rain. She could taste the moisture in the back of her mouth.

At the doors Fenella took Eleanor's other arm and pulled her aside, whispering as they entered. Hannah caught only the first line of Fenella's words, *"Me brother asks that ye find him during prayers."* Hannah was excited for Eleanor. She knew her friend was in love with the Highlander, but there couldn't possibly be a match between them. Eleanor was destined to be betrothed to King George … if and when Queen Charlotte died. Or was murdered.

The contemplation of such a horrid political plan seemed twice as evil as she walked toward a pew, under the gaze of the saints on the stained-glass windows.

Hannah peered around at the parishioners in attendance. Behind her, at the far wall, stood the McKelvey men. One gave her a quick nod and she blushed. The pew she intended to sit in, next to Eleanor, was full. She found a spot in the next pew behind her good friend. She sat, tightened the bow on her bonnet, and smoothed a wrinkle on the apron front of her skirt.

The vicar, dressed in a long robe, passed up the aisle. He looked to be about a hundred years old. He carried a candle and an incense shaker. A floral note with a hint of resin reached Hannah's nose.

Directly in front of her the Baroness cocked her head toward Eleanor. "My dear," she whispered, "you don't look well."

Hannah leaned forward about to offer to help Eleanor out of the church, but the Baroness clicked her fingers at her daughter-in-law. "Could you take her out for some air, Fenella?"

Hannah smirked. She wasn't stupid. Fenella would help Eleanor meet up with Keir. They weren't even waiting for prayers.

3

The service began soon after Fenella returned to her seat. Hannah heard her explain to the Baroness that Eleanor was ill and one of her brothers was escorting her back to Beldorney Hall. Hannah chanced to peek around. There were only two McKelveys standing with the carriage drivers at the back of the sanctuary. Her own heart beat a little faster and heat rose up her neck at the thought of Eleanor alone with Keir. She braced herself for the fact that she might have just lost her friend forever. Eleanor had almost run away without her last night and Hannah had feared for her, but now … if she was with Keir …

Hannah pondered the problem through prayers. What if she ran away with Keir? What if she was really sick?

If they showed up at the ball tonight, fine. If they didn't, well, Hannah could impersonate a princess and take her place. She doubled up on her praying then, thinking what the rewards might be for her if she took Eleanor's place.

***

LOGAN AND JACK stood fidgeting at the back of the sanctuary. They were used to sitting in the front pew at the larger hilltop kirk the McKelveys frequented, but standing here in this unfamiliar kirk for a couple of hours meant restless mischief now that Keir had gone out.

"'Tis rainin'," Jack whispered, giving his brother a tug on his kilt. "'Twon't be long and the princess'll be scramblin' to come inside." He raised a brow at his brother. The gravelly voice of the vicar rose and fell with a regular rhythm, his words intelligible only on the high notes.

Logan matched the facial expression, shoved a quiet elbow into Jack's side, while his green eyes glinted in the candlelight. The room grew darker as the clouds outside lowered. "Ye willna see her till tonight or mayhaps nivver ag'in." The patter of heavy rain began.

"Nivver?" Jack frowned.

"Aye," Logan nodded for Jack to follow. They slipped out the door they'd recently held open for Fenella's return and Keir's quick exit. Sheltered under a modest overhang, Logan spoke in a normal tone, "Aye, ye ken our brother. He's on a mission."

"I ken. I heard ye speakin' o' the plot last night. First he was to marry her off to King George, then poison her, and now … what? Run off with her sittin' on the back o' Copper?" Jack blew air out his lips, flapping them in suspicion.

4

Logan placed a hand on Jack's shoulder as the first crack of lightning lit the sky. "Nay. He'll be ridin' Copper and the princess'll sit on me new mare, the prize I won from McDoon." The thunder punctuated his statement. He cringed and added, "I'll be ridin' back to Beldorney Hall in the carriage." He smirked. "With the … lass … Hannah."

Jack gave him a punch hard enough to send Logan stumbling into the rain. Another lightning strike and clap of thunder added to the skirmish. Logan responded and soon they were tussling in the mud like young lads.

"They'll nay let ye in the carriage now," Jack huffed when they finally ended their impromptu fight. He ambled off to his horse, saluted Logan, and galloped away.

Logan snorted and put his face toward the heavens. The rain felt cold, but did a fair job of washing the mud down. He was still dripping an hour later when the service ended and the parishioners scurried out to their coaches.

"Captain!" he shouted at the red-coated gentleman who was directing a carriage to come nearer to the entryway. "Me brother has tended to the princess and I am without me mare. I beg a chance to ride in yer carriage."

Luxbury stopped short, eyed Logan from head to heel, and managed to make his eyebrows meet above his sharp nose. "You're sopping wet, man. And what's this about Eleanor? Is she not in the carriage already?" He waved faster at the driver who had to wait for another coach to move.

"Sir," Logan cocked his head trying to look subservient, or at least convivial, "The lady was ill and Keir took her back to—"

He couldn't finish before Luxbury grabbed at him, gave him a shake, and roared in his face, "What? The princess rode off with that … that …" He growled an oath and gritted his teeth.

Passing parishioners scowled at him. Fenella, with her son, husband, and the Beldorneys, looked away. Hannah came out next.

"Logan, what happened to you?" She glanced at Luxbury and then at the carriage that pulled up close.

"Me own form of baptism, m'lady," Logan joked.

Luxbury opened the carriage door, looked inside, and turned. "She's not here."

"I told ye," Logan said, "Princess Nora took ill. Me brother has seen to her comfort. She's well cared for, captain."

5

Luxbury held out a hand to help Hannah step up. She settled in and Luxbury followed her with a curt warning to Logan. "There's no room for you, boy, but you can hang onto the back step like a footman."

"Oh, Bernard, let him come in." Hannah pushed on the door that Luxbury was trying to pull closed. "He can sit next to me if you're afraid of ruining that fine wool coat."

The smile she offered Logan made him speechless. The very first time he'd seen her at the Beldorneys' he'd been struck dumb. He knew that Pascoe and Hannah were one and the same, a lad dressed up now like a girl, but she, or rather he, was almost too convincing. He stifled a laugh as he stared. *The captain doesn't ken the truth, nor does me brother, Jack. 'Twill be me best trick to get one or both to fall in love wi' Pascoe.*

"Well, get in, Logan. You are most welcome to ride with us." Hannah scooted to the side to allow him room. "And Bernard, tell the driver to hurry. I want to check on, uh, Princess Nora."

Logan melted into the spot Hannah allowed and whispered to her. "Thank ye, Pascoe."

***

HANNAH SHIVERED WHEN Logan called her by her last name. *He still thinks I'm a boy. But Bernard, of course, knows I'm a young woman and not a disguised English lad, made to play-act at fooling the guests and the princess.* Her mind raced through all the times she'd been with Logan since coming to Scotland. She'd met him first when she and Eleanor were wearing boys' clothes and pretending to be the accomplices hired to aid in a plot against Eleanor herself. Only Fenella had guessed their true gender and kept their secret. The McKelveys decided to dress them up as females, better to infiltrate the royals, never suspecting that Eleanor was the secret princess and Hannah her best friend. Logan completely believed Hannah was a lad now dressed as a lass.

Her mind raced through the implications. A grudging curve on her lips appeared where a smile should have been. "You're welcome, Master McKelvey."

She often joined in harmless pranks with the lads at Ingledew as she grew up there and now, perhaps to lessen the stress of the current situation, it occurred to her how delightful it might be to trifle with the affections of a certain young man as well as his very attractive younger brother. She might even use the captain in the slightly perverse scheme that formed in the back of her mind.

Luxbury filled the other seat of the carriage, harrumphing and snorting like the pompous snob he was.

She reached across and patted his hand. With another of her charming smiles she said, "Did you enjoy the vicar's homily, Bernard?"

His eyes darted from her hand to the wet lad whose presence he had to bear and back to her eyes. "Why, why yes, Hannah. Though parts seemed to be more of a harangue than a homily."

"'Twas good," Logan butted in, "'cept fer when he misquoted the Lord."

Luxbury's head swiveled and he looked down his nose at Logan. "And how would you know that?"

"Me dear departed mum was accustomed to reading the Holy Word to us younguns every day. We memorized a goodly portion." Logan pressed a hand to the ceiling for balance as the coach lurched forward.

"Well, if your brother Keir had listened to such teachings, he wouldn't have taken off alone with Princess Nora. I wonder whose coach he stole."

Hannah glanced at Logan to see how he'd defend his brother, but Logan only gazed closed-mouth at the captain and started a new conversation about swords and pistols and the training of English soldiers. Bernard fell into a new argument that showed his own obvious lack of knowledge in Scottish weaponry.

Hannah made the appropriate feminine responses at the right times, savoring the moments when she knew her comments were perceived by the captain as foolishly girlish, while at the same time she could see that Logan thought her words were cleverly girlish, since he believed she was a he. She wrinkled her nose once or twice as the captain's wool coat began to stink with a wet dog smell.

When they reached Beldorney Hall the captain remembered his manners and allowed Logan, an invited guest, to climb out first and help Hannah.

"Ah, the rain has stopped," Luxbury said. "Hannah, I'll be in my room. Please send me word of how our little princess is feeling."

"Of course, I'm sure she'll be fine." Hannah gave a stilted curtsy, knowing Bernard would think she was still learning what she'd been sent here to learn, and Logan would think the lad, Pascoe, was brutishly impersonating a lady.

Luxbury walked off and Logan lowered his voice to say, "Ye're gettin' too guid at yer deceptions, Pascoe. The captain is well fooled. Tell me, are ye gettin' any looks under Princess Nora's skirts? And, hey-o, I almost fergot. I havnae seen yer cohort, El. Are they keepin' 'im in the kitchen?"

So, Keir hasn't had a chance to tell him. He doesn't know that El is really Eleanor and Eleanor is really and truly Princess Nora.

"Uh, I don't know. I haven't seen El in a while. Maybe he ran off."

"Twice the payout fer ye, then." He gave her a hearty shove and laughed.

Hannah rubbed her arm where he'd made contact and swallowed a high note of surprise. Despite being attracted to him, she also found him a bit of a boor at times.

Jack suddenly appeared and shouted at Logan.

"Have ye lost yer mind, Logan? Ye cannae touch a lady like she were a misbehavin' mare." He marched up, his facial expression easy to read. "Are ye all right, Mistress Hannah?"

Hannah hid her amusement as two possible responses formed in her mind. She chose the second, put a hand to her forehead as if she were about to faint, and sighed. "I've never been assaulted by a gentleman, but … but … I'm sure your brother meant nothing by it. Perhaps he only slipped in those sodden boots and was reaching out to balance himself." She fluttered her lashes at Logan and then at Jack as she lowered her hand. "Thank you for your concern, Jack." She leaned forward and laid a quiet kiss on his cheek.

She deduced both boys' reactions as their faces betrayed them. Jack lifted his chin up and gave Logan a look of triumph while Logan snickered and shot a conspiratorial smile at Hannah. She liked having a secret between them, but it was the wrong secret.

***

HANNAH HURRIED UP to Eleanor's room. The door was open and a maid was tending to the fire and another was laying out luncheon things.

8

"Where is Princess Nora?" she asked them, breathing in both the comforting scents of burning oak and warm bread.

She'd startled the girl at the hearth who tipped back on her bum and clasped a hand to her chest. The other, at the small table, looked up and answered, "Guid mornin', Miss, the Princess went to the master's kirk. Did ye nay go with them?"

"Yes, but ... but she left ... ill. She hasn't arrived?"

She shook her head. The one at the fire said, "I carried the tinder in and saw nary a soul return before the Baron and the Baroness. Could she have been in their carriage?"

"No." Hannah frowned and went back into the hall.

A horrible thought took hold and nearly choked her. She eyed the McKelveys' room across the hall. Would ...? No, impossible. Eleanor would never ... But Keir had uncovered her secret by accident, seen her bare bosom, learned in the most embarrassing way that she was not a he.

She stared at the door, but then a maid came out of the McKelvey room, carrying an empty tray. The lass curtsied at Hannah.

"Wait ... is anyone in there?"

"Nay, miss, the lads havnae returned. I just set out their loaves and cheeses." She curtsied again and limped away.

Hannah paced the hall, started for the servants' staircase, and heard the huffing breath of Mrs. Perkins ascending. The woman was the first person she and Eleanor confessed their true identities to, an English woman, head of the household servants.

"Mrs. Perkins, I cannot find Eleanor. She became ill and left the kirk with Keir McKelvey. Have you seen them?"

The woman, her face damp with the effort of climbing so many steps, her arms laden with linens, answered, "My, my, no. I'm just bringing these fresh things to the master's son's room. I haven't seen a soul but the lovely Fenella." She lowered her voice to a whisper. "She was mortified that young Huey wet the sheets. 'Twill be a secret best kept from the Baroness." She tittered.

"Perhaps Fenella knows. Could you tell me which way to her rooms?"

"Follow me."

Hannah was relieved to find Fenella alone and learned that Hubert and Huey had gone hunting with the Baron and the male guests while the women lunched, rested, and readied themselves for the evening's activities.

"I cannot find Eleanor. There'll be no ball for the Princess if there's no Princess." Hannah flung her arms, audibly exhaling.

Fenella patted her middle and plopped into a chair. "Och, dinnae fash, Hannah. Me brother Keir has proposed to the lass."

"Proposed?" Hannah took a seat at the window.

"Aye, and by her absence I ken her answer. She's eloped wi' the lad. He's saved her from her nasty fate and himself from that heartless MacLeod lass."

"Eloped? Eleanor and Keir?" Hannah's brows knitted more tightly together as she stared slack-jawed at Fenella.

"'Twould be a terrible shame fer me husband's family to cancel the ball. 'Twas a bit upsettin' to the Baroness to have Eleanor leave the banquet last night. But I've been athinkin'. Ye left early as well and so there could surely be some confusion aboot the two of ye. I believe we can still have the ball and give them a princess … ye can wear the wig Eleanor used and dress in the purple gown I ken she planned to wear tonight."

Stunned further, Hannah closed her eyes. She could do it; she was not Eleanor's equal, but in her heart she knew she was every bit as headstrong and willful, though she had no royal blood running through her veins. But she was brave, perhaps not as brave as Eleanor around snakes and spiders, but … ah, the fun it would be to have all eyes on her, just as she had so recently fantasized … and Jack and Logan would be in on the deception, but each in a different way.

She opened her eyes to see Fenella, her head cocked and a worried expression on her face. "I'll do it. But only if the Baroness approves … and your other brothers must be my only dance partners."

Fenella's grin split her face. "Ah, they're quite the rascals and I've seen the way they look at ye. I'll make 'em mind their manners and hold the secret. I can only think of one problem we may have. That captain. I ken the plan was to murder the queen and then marry Eleanor off to the king … ye'll nay hafta go so far, but Captain Luxbury may have other thoughts."

"I'll speak to him." Hannah rose. "I'll go now. He's expecting a word from me about Eleanor's health."

Chapter 2

THE BARONESS STOOD in Eleanor's room and puckered her brow at Hannah.

"Don't worry, dear, 'tis good ye told him and better still that he's in pursuit. I'm sure the captain and his men will find them and ye willna hafta bear such a burden fer us and fer yer friend as to take her place. 'Tis a true service ye'd be doin' though." She moved as if to leave the chambers, put her shoulders back, and spoke more formally. "I did not want to be involved in this insurrectionist plot. I blame the Baron, our relatives in England, and Bernard. If Eleanor truly did run away … well, no matter. We will get through this. I'm very grateful for your help, Hannah. Mrs. Perkins and Carla will assist you in your preparations." She spun around and spoke to Mrs. Perkins. "There's a veil in me daughter's trunk. If ye can dye it to match before tonight, I think that will help disguise Hannah and confuse anyone who got a good look at her last night."

"Yes, ma'am. She'll be our princess should the English soldiers not bring the real one back in time."

"Mm, yes. An amendment to our own little Cendrillon story." The Baroness gave Hannah a humorless smile. She swished her skirts as she did the closest thing to stomping out of the room that was allowed by her station in life.

Hannah bit her lip and put herself to the task of becoming a princess. If only Eleanor were here …

She chuckled to herself remembering a time when the two of them were forbidden to attend an Ingledew ball. They had spied from under the tables set up behind the musicians. She hadn't minded being remanded to the stables—she loved horses as much as Eleanor did—but her greatest wish was to attend a ball. *I'm going to do this.* She had tested her acting ability several times in the last few weeks, fooling people into thinking she was a boy, or a boy pretending to be a girl, or a maid, or that she was ignorant at reading … and she had even fooled Eleanor when Bernard had given them dancing lessons. She pretended to be clumsy so Eleanor would look all the better.

She eyed the purple gown laid out on Eleanor's bed and wished for half a second that she hadn't burned the smelly boys' clothes they'd first worn. *No, I'll not run away.* The thought of dancing with Logan and Jack was too appealing. She had put Eleanor first for as long as she remembered; she was finally getting a chance to be somebody important.

She began the long process of getting ready. The wig she wore was made of hair much darker than hers; the maid, Carla, tucked the blonde wisps under as Hannah assessed herself in the mirror. A little darkening of her pale eyebrows made the transformation complete. She looked far more like Eleanor than she looked like herself–Hannah Pascoe. And the purple veil Mrs. Perkins brought in gave the right amount of mystery to her countenance, making her smile and eyes more enigmatic.

A knock at the door sent Carla rushing to answer. Fenella walked in with another woman and Carla slipped out.

"This be me sister, Elsie," she said. The two red-haired beauties were dressed in beautiful gowns of complimentary shades of green. "And she kens all the special details aboot ye, dressin' as a lad and foolin' the men-folk."

Hannah lifted the veil, stood, and curtsied. "I'm most pleased to meet you. I've heard a few things from Logan about his sisters."

Their laughter was musical. "Did he tell ye he bet a McDoon he could beat him in a horse race? And if he lost, he woulda showed'im our sister Rory's knickers?" Elsie said. "He's lucky I'm all trussed up and too fine a lady tonight to wallop the daylights outta 'f'im."

Hannah smiled along with them. "I did hear of the race and I've ridden the horse he won."

Fenella nodded. "Aye, let me tell me sister. Hannah rode double with our Logan, dressed as a lad. And he doesna ken the truth of her womanliness, but thinks the lad and Hannah are two different Sassenachs."

Hannah lowered her eyes a moment, hesitant to confess something more, then took courage when Fenella said, "We should inspire the wee lads, both Logan and Jack, to fall in love."

"I'm afraid I am guilty of … well, Logan thinks I'm a boy and Jack has only seen me as a girl. I believe Logan is bent on persuading Jack to woo me and then intends to spoil things with what he thinks is the truth."

Elsie laughed louder than Fenella. "'Twould serve him right. Perhaps I'll let the wee Jack in on the stunt his brother means. The joke will be on Logan."

Hannah swallowed hard and confessed, "I rather like Logan. It was only a fleeting amusement I even considered playing them off each other." She brought the veil back down over her face. "I do not want to hurt the feelings of either of your brothers."

The door opened a crack and Carla apologized for interrupting, "So sorry, m'ladies, but the Baroness has asked fer yer presence below. I'm to wait with the … the princess."

***

NEW GUESTS ARRIVED and crowded the main hall. The overnight guests made their entrances down the grand staircase as did the two McKelvey sisters, and there they mingled, telling the recent arrivals of the princess's beauty and fragile constitution. How she seemed to float as she walked, but was obviously weak and in delicate health. How she'd smiled warmly and how honored they were to speak a word or two with her the previous evening.

Without the captain to escort Hannah from the top of the stairs, she appeared alone at the railing. The Baron stood on the steps at the midpoint to finish the entrance with her on his arm. All eyes looked up.

Fenella, standing near her brothers, nudged Logan. "Go help the lass down, will ye?"

Jack heard too and started off first. The competition was on. Both lads rushed past the Baron and bolted up the steps. There were gasps from the ladies below, fans fluttered, and men cleared their throats. It took but seconds for the McKelveys to reach Hannah, having taken the steps two and three at a time. On the landing Logan bowed and then Jack bowed lower and upon rising took her hand. Logan glared at this brother and held an arm out on Hannah's other side, framing her with their tartan colors, the reds clashing with the purple. She slipped her hand through the crook of his elbow and smiled at him. She turned her head back to Jack and gave him an equally engaging grin. He raised her hand to his lips and kissed it.

"Thank you, Jack." She drew her hand back and then slipped it through his arm. "Shall we go down?"

The guests were not silent. Kind and gracious words reached Hannah's ears. She kept her head up, afraid to tilt it too much and lose the wig. The veil did as much to hide her face as it did to hinder her vision. She relied completely on the men at her sides to guide her down the stone staircase. She missed a step, but no one noticed as Jack and Logan kept her steady and she felt as if she were floating down. The Baron gave a nod where he stood midway, and a wave of his arm to allow the boys to continue escorting her themselves. He stepped to one side to let them pass.

When they reached the last step, the Baroness came forward and held her hands out to Hannah, palms up.

She raised her voice for all to hear her announce, "Princess Nora, everyone." There was muted clapping from gloved hands.

Hannah released her grip on the McKelveys' strong forearms and clasped the Baroness's fingers and leaned forward, head still stiffly held high. The Baroness pressed her cheek against Hannah's veiled face in a more intimate yet respectful greeting.

"Allow me to introduce you to our newest guests." Light from hundreds of candles made the Baroness's eyes sparkle. "Come with me, Princess."

***

JACK LET HIS breath out and watched Hannah—pretending to be a princess—magically glide through the crowd and mesmerize men and women alike. Logan nudged him covertly by touching the hilt of his sword and making the pointed end tap his brother's kilted thigh. It was enough to break Jack's concentration and he scowled at Logan.

"Ye spoilt things by followin' me up the stairs. I was all the lady needed." Jack complained.

Logan let a gruff laugh spill out of his lips, quietly though, as the MacLeod clan was near. "Fenella's command was fer me, brother, ye were the one doin' the followin'. Ye best lower yer expectations. I ken fer a fact that father is negotiatin' a dowry wi' the McDoons. Their wee Megan will be of age the summer next. She'll make ye a fine wife wi' those rounded hips."

Jack gritted his teeth and narrowed his eyes, ready to take on his brother in a louder and more physical altercation. Then he thought of his older brother, Keir, and knew what he would do: ignore the provocation and let this fire die out. Logan was surely lying; there was no such negotiation or his father, Laird Finley McKelvey of Castle Caladh, would have come to this gala.

Hannah was through the crowd about to enter the grand ballroom. There'll be dancing, Jack thought, something he was better at than Logan. He stepped back and let Logan go ahead, then quickly skirted around the edge of the room and entered the ballroom ahead of his brother and sisters.

Chairs lines the walls; the scent of fresh spring flowers overwhelmed the waxy candle smoke, aided by the various perfumes the guests wore. The musicians were already playing a slow ballad. Jack locked eyes with Hannah, or at least he believed she was looking at him. The veil obscured her expression, but he wanted to believe she was giving him a silent request to come to her. He strode confidently to her side.

"M'lady, may I have the honor of the first dance?"

***

LOGAN STIFLED A snort when he saw Jack move with Pascoe to the dance floor. If Jack knew he was dancing with a common English lad he'd be humiliated. He couldn't wait to see the look on Jack's face when he found out. Unfortunately, it wouldn't be tonight.

15

Logan scanned the other couples that danced. He saw Anabel MacLeod on the arm of Dylan McDoon. *Och, he's nay wastin' time puttin' his boots where Keir's should be.*

Anabel was a beauty, no doubt the bonniest lass in the Highlands. She was Keir's betrothed, according to their father, but not as far as Keir was concerned. Logan wondered where Keir might be now—with the real princess—and what they might be doing. Anabel and Dylan swished by close to him and he caught her flowery scent. She was a prize even if Keir was right about her being quarrelsome and contrary. Well, perhaps someone—someone like him—could tame her. He didn't let himself think further other than to continue admiring her lovely red hair, her pert nose, and winsome smile. She danced well enough and seemed to enjoy Dylan's attention.

Jack and the false princess swung by next and Logan smirked. The smile beaming from Jack's face was real. The lad was smitten with Pascoe. A jolt of remorse hit Logan, and pity for his brother. He'd have to tell him sooner rather than later that this substitute princess was a lad.

Pascoe caught his eye and Logan's heart skipped a beat. *Nay, he cannae be castin' a woman's spell on me.* He forced himself to watch them twirl about the room. He calmed a bit until they circled back near him and it was easier to see her face behind the veil. No, *his* face. He liked Pascoe; he liked him as Hannah; and now he liked him in a curious and strange way as a princess whose enchanting countenance captivated him. *What evil spell is this?*

He shook his head and squeezed his eyes shut for a moment. The music stopped and the dancers stepped toward the table set with goblets filled with water or wine. He watched his brother speak to Pascoe, touch her—*his*—hand, gesture toward the refreshments, and lead her—*nay, him*—there.

Fenella came out of nowhere and whispered in his ear. "She truly looks like a princess, aye?"

"*He!*" Logan hissed back.

"Nay … *she* … and ye best keep yer voice low. Now get yerself over there and dance wi' the *lady*."

"The devil take ye; I willna do such a thing."

"Jack'll wonder why ye dinnae try to outdo 'im."

16

Logan ignored the pounding in his chest. His sister was right; he needed to challenge his younger brother or Jack might figure out the ruse and ruin the night with a strong reaction the others would witness. He crossed the room. This would be difficult, but he'd have to dance with Pascoe as many times as Jack. Perhaps he could vary the night by partnering with Anabel or one of the other young ladies. His eyes darted around the room, noting that no other girl or woman compared to Anabel's exquisite good looks … except Pascoe. All right, he'd have to think of *him* as Hannah … no, as Princess Nora. He'd close his eyes and imagine the real princess.

***

HANNAH WAS GIDDY. First Jack and then Logan danced with her. She didn't miss a step. The lads were far better than her minuet teacher, the stuffy Captain Luxbury, who she was quite glad wasn't here. She'd given him a false trail to follow, telling him she was certain Keir had taken Eleanor to Castle Caladh. The truth was Eleanor wanted to find her mother and the only clue they had was from Fenella. She wasn't about to tell the captain that.

A handsome young man approached, a McDoon she thought, intent on leading her for the third dance, but Jack stepped in front of him, whisking her back to the dance floor. The evening continued in like manner with Jack attending her like a besotted suitor, and Logan taking his place quite often. There were other young men and several older ones who tried to catch her attention, but she succeeded in waving them off or at least speaking a word or two before reaching for Jack's arm or Logan's.

The evening passed in a blur, ending with a feast with her sitting where Eleanor had sat the night before. She was famished, but she'd have to lift the veil to eat and reveal her less than royal features. Perhaps those sitting to the right or across from her might detect the ruse.

The footmen poured the wine and the guests watched and waited for her to raise her glass.

"I can't do it," she whispered to the Baroness, her fingers on the goblet's stem.

"Just one sip," her hostess whispered back.

Hannah raised the goblet with one hand and placed her other hand on the front edge of the veil. All the guests raised their cups, smiling, watching.

"To the princess!" the Baron shouted.

The crowd roared the words back and drank. Hannah slipped the goblet under the veil and drank more than she should have. She let the veil drop back and set the goblet down. The servants stepped forward with platters and trays and began serving. Hannah leaned toward the Baroness.

"I don't feel well."

"I'll see you up myself," she answered, signaling the closest servant to move back.

Her abrupt departure was accepted by the ladies and gentlemen who'd witnessed a similar retreat from the real princess the night before. They began to gossip with the newer guests about the princess's delicate constitution.

"Are you truly unwell?" the Baroness asked when they reached the staircase where wisps of smoke from the dozens of candles that had been snuffed still lingered.

"I did not want to fold back the veil." Hannah looked down at the first step and instantly put her hands up to catch her wig which was slipping forward.

"I understand. Well, ye'll be off to England soon. We've had word that Queen Charlotte is with child again. Surely she'll succumb to some unfortunate birthing injury and ye must be in place when she dies … to comfort the King."

"Me?" Hannah dropped one hand to grab the railing.

"Well, only if Eleanor doesn't return. Ye've taken her place. 'Tis expected. Ye'll be fine, lass." The Baroness began the climb.

Hannah's frown froze on her face. She couldn't move.

"Come along." The Baroness stared back. "Oh, ye poor thing. Ye've misunderstood the timing. Ye'll be stayin' here a few weeks more, until we hear of the Queen's demise, and then there'll be the mournin'. Aye, ye'll be with us all the summer, I expect. And surely by then that rascal McKelvey'll bring Nora back or else Bernard will. Do ye feel better?" She took another step up, sniffed. "Come along before the smoke makes ye faint."

Hannah managed a step and then another, but it was her hand pulling her up the railing rather than her reluctant feet. She'd rather shed the wig, lift her hem, run to the stable, leap on Logan's mare and race away. North, south, it didn't matter. She stopped climbing. The Baroness snapped her fingers and uttered a short command to someone Hannah couldn't see. Her eyes were glued to her hand on the rail, her mind caught in indecision, her feet too heavy to lift.

Then whispering, fleecy and soft, brushed past her ears.

"We have no smellin' salts. Just lift her."

"Should I carry … her … up to her room?"

"Yes, yes, hurry. I fear she'll faint away."

She was sure one whisperer was the Baroness, but the other was a male voice. Why was it that men could never whisper like women could? The hoarse words coated the nearer ear.

"I've got ye. Let go of the rail."

She knew who it was then. His scent, his touch. She'd danced with him all night. Her fingers let go of the rail.

His arm was around her. He lifted her. She closed her eyes, let her wig rest upon his shoulder. Best if she said nothing. Pretend to faint?

The Baroness's instructions to her rescuer were short: take her to Eleanor's room; put her on the settee. The Baroness huffed and puffed behind them, then at the top of the landing, she went ahead down the hall to open the door.

***

LOGAN FELT SORRY for the lad in his arms, light as a feather, all dressed up in purple, wigged and powdered to impersonate a female. Clever child, though, to repeat the charade of illness the same as the night before, though he wondered how the lad knew of it. At the top of the stairs, he followed the Baroness, the warmth of Pascoe's face against his chest a strange distraction. He shouldn't have left the feast, but he couldn't let Jack best him. Jack was out of his seat and ready to race after the pretend princess. He'd had to jerk the lad back into his seat and use a threat he knew would work. He strode out of the dining hall through a different door and then found his way around to the main stairs.

When he saw Pascoe falter on the steps, he almost believed the lad was indeed a lass. He rushed up without thinking and caught the poor thing before the imminent collapse.

Maybe the boy really was ill … or planning to run off. Did Keir already pay Pascoe? Did he give him El's portion as well? It was rather strange how Pascoe claimed he hadn't seen El in a while and suggested he might have run away.

He looked down at the delicate features. Pascoe's eyelids fluttered. He noted the darkened brows, smudged as the veil tightened, caught between her face—*his* face—and Logan's chest.

"Take her to Princess Nora's room and put her on the settee."

Logan followed the Baroness, entered the room, considered briefly dropping the lad hard on the settee, but it must have been that glass of wine, drunk quickly, that colored his logic, for he couldn't make himself be anything but gentle with the soft body in his arms.

"I need to get back to me guests. 'Tisn't proper to leave ye alone with her, but … as ye're a McDoon I'll—"

"Nay, I'm a McKelvey, through and through."

The Baroness's hands flew to her mouth and Logan was instantly sorry he'd spoken.

"Brother to me son's wife?"

"Aye, Baroness, ye welcomed us here yerself."

"And brother to the McKelvey who has ruined me husband's plans and carried off the real princess?" She put both hands on her forehead and mumbled, "What have I wrought? By not accepting Fenella sooner I've made enemies of her family."

"Aye, I mean, nay. That is … 'twas me brother … but he means only to help … ye have steadfast friends among us McKelveys. There be others who wish to spoil things. I believe he's protectin' the princess, whether helpin' her in some way, or chasin' after the real kidnappers … if that's what's become of her." He glanced at Pascoe's still frame. The veil fluttered with the rise and fall of a very round bosom. His thoughts fled from his brain and he stared too long.

"All right then." The Baroness took a settling breath. "I must get back to the dinner." She put a firm hand against his chest. "I'll be sendin' Mrs. Perkins on the run. I'm only lettin' ye stay because this poor lass has saved us from disgrace and dishonor and we owe her our constant attention. See she doesn't choke … the state she's in I … oh!" She threw her hands up and twirled on her heel. At the door she added, "See she doesn't slump down or bite her tongue."

20

The moment she disappeared he turned to Hannah and knelt, shook her knee, and tapped her cheek.

"Pascoe ... she's gone ... ye can open yer eyes now. I ken ye're jist play-actin'."

Hannah's head lolled to one side and the wig fell off, the veil going with it. A tiny smirk grew on her lips.

"Ye big fake," Logan growled. He squeezed the knee hard and Hannah yelped. "Ye even sound like a lass."

Hannah sat up straight. "Maybe the fairies changed me. What if I were a princess ... or just a plain lady ... a maid even. Would you find me ... desirable?"

Logan swatted her knee and stood. "Nay, what's wrong wi' ye, Pascoe? Have ye been wearin' the lace and the bonnets and the underclothes all these weeks to yer detriment?" He started to pace the room, but stopped at the fireplace and stared at the embers.

Stomping footsteps preceded the entrance of Mrs. Perkins. "Out, young man. You don't want to miss the second course. I'll see to the princess now."

"But ye ken she's nay—"

"Out. I'm the housekeeper and there be no secrets kept from me. I know everything." She winked at Logan and he scowled back.

Ah, she does ken. The scowl left his face. He felt better, but thought he should check the stables and see if El was there after all.

Chapter 3

T WAS UNEXPECTED, FER sure," Fenella admitted to Hannah. She sat near the hearth in Hannah's room, her shoes off, warming her toes on this unexpectedly chilly morning. "I believe me brother Keir to be upstandin' in his thoughts and deeds. Our mother taught us well. He had two plans. One was to have Eleanor dress again in those lad's clothes ye first showed up in and lend her a horse to go in search of her mother. If she had agreed, she could have gone today, and not missed last night's ball. The other plan also included a search for her mother, with a slight variation." She snickered and brought one foot to her lap to rub her arches. "I kent he rode out to the kirk before dawn yesterday and met with the vicar. He arranged a private weddin' should Eleanor agree. 'Twould solve his own trouble of bein' hitched to Anabel and he could travel openly with Eleanor as his wife. They would leave immediately and miss the ball." She switched feet and watched Hannah's expression change. "'Tis evident which plan she chose. He's in love with her, ye ken."

Hannah nodded. "And she with him, but … to marry him? So suddenly? And I … I wonder at her leaving me behind. We've never been apart as long as I can remember."

"Love makes one do things ye think ye'll nivver do." She set her foot down and clasped her hands over her rounded belly. "I once vowed nivver to step foot in Beldorney Hall. Yet here I am."

"Do you think Eleanor and Keir will return once they find her mother? Or will they have to hide forever … from the insurrectionists they're betraying?"

"There's nay betrayal yet, thanks to ye, Hannah."

"Oh … I see … but …"

"Dinnae fash, I've newly acquired some persuasiveness with me mother-in-law." She patted her middle. "I'll convince her to let Hubert and me take ye to Castle Caladh. We have to deliver me brothers Jack and Logan safely home and since Keir took Logan's mare, and Jack refuses to ride double, we'll have our own attentive footman clinging to the back." The thought amused her, it seemed.

Hannah smiled slightly. "I think you should let Logan know the truth."

"Och," Fenella said, sounding like her brother, "I've dropped enough hints on his thick head. Let him figure it out on his own."

"But not like Keir did."

Fenella cocked her head, curious, and Hannah, in a less than timid manner, reported how Keir had unwittingly pulled off Eleanor's shirt.

"Oh, saints be!" Fenella covered her mouth with her hand, then began laughing uproariously. "I'll drop a few more hints."

***

THERE WAS MUCH commotion in the courtyard upon the departures of so many guests who'd stayed the night after the ball. Horses and carriages and footmen and servants almost outnumbered the dozens of Scots who were ready to leave at nearly the same time.

Fenella walked toward the Beldorneys' carriage with her young son, Huey, in hand and a carpet bag in the other. Hannah, stoop-shouldered, followed her like a servant with two more bags. The carriage was offered when Fenella had a pleasant breakfast with her husband's now attentive parents. Her husband, Hubert, helped Fenella up and then tossed Hannah's bags onto the roof. He helped Hannah, who was dressed plainly and doing an excellent impression of a subordinate and not a Princess, into the carriage. Lastly, he scooped up Huey and planted him next to Fenella. A few feet away, Jack held the reins of his own horse as well as the carriage's two geldings which were prancing in place.

"Ready, then?" Hubert spoke to his wife, his hand about to close the carriage door.

"Nay, we must wait fer Logan. There's space enough next to Hannah."

Hubert nodded and glanced back toward the manse's arched entrance. Anabel MacLeod stood there blocking Logan's path. Her words, spoken too loudly for well-bred manners, fell on their ears like lambs bleating.

Anabel screeched, "Where did Keir go? And what happened to that mousy maid that tended the Princess? Tell me, Logan McKelvey. Did the scoundrel run off with her?"

Logan went red-faced and how he answered did not appease Anabel, though whatever he said was low, polite, and respectful.

"Helping her? Why would he help a maid?" Her voice still fell loud and squeaky on the ears of all in the courtyard. The frown she made turned her lovely features into a shrewish mask. An attending maid came forth holding a basket for Anabel. "Get away from me," she shouted at the poor servant. "You've been a nuisance for three days. Give me that."

Logan used the distraction to stride around Anabel and head quickly for the carriage. He pulled open the door, put one foot up to lunge in, saw the only space was next to Hannah, and said, "Och, I dinnae expect ye to be here." He looked from her to his sister.

"We're takin' her to Caladh. Get in afore that fearsome wench takes her wrath out on yer back. Sit there." Fenella pointed.

Hannah smiled at him and moved over an inch more. The smile sent his head into a spin. It was many miles to Castle Caladh and the thought of sitting so close to the lad, who was smiling and looking far more charming and fetching at this moment than the beautiful Anabel, made his mouth go dry and the words he might have said vanished into thin air.

Fenella reached a hand out and slapped his shoulder. "Ye're gawkin', Logan. Get in or get out."

He finished his entrance, ducking and pouring his large frame into the tight space, his kilt settling stiff and scratchy on his thighs, his elbow touching Hannah's. Her fresh and very womanly scent filled his nostrils. She must have just bathed. *He! He* must have just bathed. This was not going to work.

"Och, 'tis too close fer … fer a lady to bear. I'll ride the back step … like a footman."

He was out and climbing onto the back of the carriage in a matter of seconds. He gripped a handle there and held on as Hubert slapped the horses' rumps and the carriage rolled forward. Logan peered back at Anabel who was still in an agitated state. Her mother appeared and put an arm around her; Anabel openly wept. With three older sisters Logan had endured his unfair share of various feminine moods; a pinch of sympathy colored his feelings for Anabel. She had a right to be sad or angry or confused because of his brother Keir's actions.

Och, there's Dylan McDoon striding to her side. She'd get a proper amount of manly attention now. All thoughts of Anabel dissipated as the carriage left the estate's cobbled drive and turned onto the bumpier dirt road. He conjured up an image of Pascoe wearing breeches and shirt. Yes, that was a better thought. Surely the lad would discard the dress and bonnet once they arrived at Castle Caladh and then maybe his uncooperative heart would beat in regular rhythm as it should.

***

HANNAH SIGHED IN disappointment. She'd hoped one of the McKelveys would have ridden inside the carriage.

"Ye like 'im, aye?" Fenella said in a whisper over her son's head. Hannah nodded. "And Jack, too?"

Another nod.

"Ye danced well on both McKelveys' arms. 'Tis hard fer me to think o' them goin' a'courtin', but they're of age. T'were but wee lads when I left Caladh to marry me Hubert. I was about the age they are now."

Hannah couldn't think of a response. She folded her hands in her lap and peered out the window. "Is it far to Castle Caladh?"

"Aye, but the time will pass quickly as we play the travelin' game me mum taught me. Do ye ken yer letters?"

"Yes."

"I've been helpin' Huey learn 'em. Now's a good time to practice." She opened the bag she'd brought and pulled out a leather-bound tome. "'Tis a gift from yer grandmother. Ye'll like this French story, Huey. It's been rewritten in English."

The journey was long, but the delightful story occupied the women and child and the game she played with the letters on the pages helped as well. Along the way they made two stops to rest the horses. Each time Jack dismounted and used the time to speak to Hannah. Logan watched and when Hannah caught him, he looked away. Once again in the coach, Hannah asked Fenella to tell Logan the truth.

"Aye, I've been honest with'im. 'Tis takin' longer for the truth to sink in, is all. No matter. I like to see the lads competin' fer yer hand. 'Tis most amusin'."

"But," Hannah lowered her voice in case Logan could hear. The carriage wheels made a lot of noise and the wood in the coach creaked, but there was no glass in the windows and Logan's perch on the back might allow him to clearly listen. "But he's suffering. I can tell."

Fenella cocked her head. "Ye're a good woman, Hannah. Ye have the same compassionate spirit as me mum had. Aye, I'll tell'im the whole story once we stop to rest the horses. We doan want'im fallin' off the back o' the coach."

***

LOGAN GAINED NEW respect for any footman obliged to bear a lengthy journey hanging on to the back end of a bouncing conveyance as he was. He was strong though and never slipped his grip or lost his footing, even when the horses lurched unexpectedly.

He could hear parts of conversations and most of the story-reading. Fenella read aloud using different voices and even accents as she entertained Huey and Pascoe. Just hearing Pascoe's faint voice brought to mind her—*his*—slight frame and feminine manners. He couldn't forget the vision of her—*him, him*—dancing around the ballroom like a real princess. He tried his best to squash the thoughts and keep an eye on the lands they were crossing, the loch, the budding trees, the fields of heather. Soon they'd come to a rather thick wood, but beyond that lay the lands he and his family knew well.

The sound of Fenella's reading faded and Logan assumed she'd either tired of reading or Huey had fallen asleep. He popped his head up from the back of the coach and hollered to Hubert. "Take care between the trees. The lane'll open in a wee bit. We're almost there."

Something off to the left drew his attention. They'd apparently scared up an animal. A deer? No, he thought he saw a horse. The carriage went through a patch of heavy brush and his view was obscured for a moment. When the carriage straightened out, he leaned precariously to see. What! Two women. Ah! One is Princess Eleanor. What a fortuitous coincidence! She saw him, but then turned her head. There was a horse and rider coming up behind her. The rider struck down the other woman and grabbed Eleanor around the waist. He pulled her up and over the saddle in front of him like a sack of potatoes.

The carriage stopped abruptly and Logan jumped down and started to run in that direction. Out of the corner of his eye he saw his brother Jack turning circles on his horse and then, coming at a run, was Keir, following or chasing a young lad. Behind him, Copper, a pack horse, and Logan's mare that Keir had borrowed, were rearing up, trying to release themselves from flimsy tethers.

Voices all around rose.

"He took her!"

"Keir! Go after them!"

And Logan himself called out, "Who's the woman? Where'd that lad come from?"

"Keir, what's going on?" Fenella cried out. She and Hannah had stepped down from the carriage and were starting to move toward the woman on the ground. "Who is that? Hello? Are you hurt?"

Logan left the injured woman to his sister's care, and changed direction to meet Keir who was still several yards away.

"Logan!" Keir then whistled for his horse. "Grab yer mare. Come. That rascal has El."

Logan caught his horse and mounted, ignoring the fact the stirrups were set too short. His mind instead whirled around the way his brother referred to Princess Nora and for a moment he wondered if there was more confusion. Had Keir found the runaway lad, El, too or did he mean Eleanor? He definitely saw Eleanor.

"Come on, Logan," Keir shouted again. "Jack, lead the pack horse to the castle."

Keir snarled a Scottish curse as he mounted Copper and said the name, "Luxbury," like a swear word. Logan followed. They couldn't gallop through the trees, but they urged their horses to go as fast as possible, reining right and left, and ducking their heads constantly.

By the time the sun set they'd wound their way west toward neighboring lands. The trails grew darker between the forests and the hills; Logan worried silently that they'd lost their prey.

Keir continually dropped epithets along the way so Logan kept his mouth closed. He knew his brother's temper and he well knew Keir had feelings for Eleanor. It was clear that was who they were following, but Logan still had questions about calling her El.

They both watched for signs of hoof prints or obscure trails. When they neared a village, Logan finally risked speaking. "The clan MacLeod lives near aboot. Could ye see yerself askin' fer their help?"

"Aye, I'd deal wi' the devil himself to get her back." Keir kept his face averted.

"Well, then, that's the path we take." Logan pointed.

Twenty minutes later Logan watched Keir tie Copper to the Mac-Leods' gate and pace up to the iron door that was locked for the night.

"They should be here by now," Logan insisted. "Our carriage left when theirs did. Anabel was makin' 'em wait, beratin' the Beldorney maid assigned to help her. We could all hear her caterwaulin' after she learnt ye were missin' along with—"

"Aye. I can jist imagine her whinin'." Keir kicked at a clump of dirt.

"Ye dinnae ken the commotion yer runnin' away wi' the princess stirred. They went ahead wi' the ball, tellin' folks Hannah, er, I mean Pascoe, was the princess." Logan cleared his throat. "I danced the whole night with the imposter. 'Twas most disconcertin' … given that I ken she's a he."

Keir looked at his brother strangely. "She coulda been the princess as easily as Eleanor."

"Aye. She was. Er, he was." He made a gravelly sound in his throat. "Fenella arranged to bring her—him—to Castle Caladh. I guess she assured Pascoe … uh … we'd find Eleanor there."

"I almost married Eleanor, Logan. But the priest died before the vows were said. 'Twas the apoplexy what took him." He quickly explained how he took Eleanor away, how Luxbury and his men intercepted them, and burned the parchment Keir planned to use to protect Eleanor. "But our clansmen sent those English buggers packin'. All except Luxbury. Our father agreed to have him go with us to search for Eleanor's mother." He snickered. "We got separated. The poor Sassenach is, per chance, in an Edinburgh jailhouse now."

Logan nodded, trying to look as though he understood it all. "And was that Eleanor's mum back in the woods?"

"Aye. And her mother's son. Did ye see who took Eleanor? 'Twas Luxbury, no?"

Logan shook his head. "It happened too fast. 'Twas some low country scoundrel."

Keir huffed and strode back to Copper and remounted. Copper gave a whinny and there was a distant answering call.

"Horses," Logan perked up. "Could be the MacLeods' carriage, now arrivin'." He gave his mare a long stroke on her neck.

A few minutes ticked by and they were rewarded with the sight of two lanterns dangling on either side of a large post-chaise driven by two men and followed by two more on horseback.

"Hullo," Keir called out, "'tis Keir McKelvey and young Logan McKelvey here at yer door. Friendly neighbors, ye ken?"

The carriage stopped and old Bram MacLeod burst out of the door.

"Ye've more nerve than an unbroke stallion showin' yer face here, McKelvey." MacLeod held the door and growled some orders to his wife and daughter inside. He slammed the door shut and faced the McKelveys. "What's yer business here in the dead of night, man?"

Keir lifted his hat and held it against his chest, his other hand on Copper's reins. "Sire … the princess … she's been abducted—"

MacLeod let loose a string of oaths before saying, "O' course we ken she's been stolen. And by me daughter's own betrothed, though that weddin' will nivver take place as long as I live. Keir McKelvey, ye've disgraced yer family name," he raised a fist, "and ye shan't find any favors among the MacLeod clan. Have ye come to find lodgin' with yer princess hoor?" He snorted in anger.

Keir opened his mouth, but Logan held up a shushing hand and twitched his gaze toward the coach where Anabel's face caught the lantern light as she poked it out the window. He wondered what she thought of her father calling Eleanor a whore.

29

Then, entranced for a moment by her beauty, he finally spoke for Keir. "Me brother was protectin' her, MacLeod. They—the English insurrectionists—meant to … to use her. Kill the queen and send Eleanor to the King's bed."

MacLeod's brow furrowed more and he lowered his fist a few inches. The darkness kept them from clearly seeing each other's eyes.

Logan went on. "Keir took her to her family … her mum … and then he was bringin' 'em to Caladh when a highwayman nabbed her. I saw it wi' me own eyes. We chased after 'em and lost the trail. Can ye spare us yer men to help us search?"

MacLeod glanced at the driver and his mate and then at the two horsemen behind the carriage, his personal guards. He answered addressing Logan and ignoring Keir, "Aye, ye can take young Will and Alpin, but give 'em time to saddle fresh mounts and raid the larder for a bite. We've been travelin' hard this day."

The driver's mate jumped down and opened the gate.

MacLeod looked to his wife and daughter whose faces were still visible, though they'd finally sat back from the window. He gave them orders to feed Logan and Keir along with their own men. To Logan and Keir he said, "Tie yer mounts at the trough and go inside, eat, and then go on yer trek. Take the lanterns." He cleared his throat and grudgingly wished them luck.

Chapter 4

ANNAH AND FENELLA fussed over Mary who was obviously hurt and confused. They insisted that she and the lad, Colin, sit inside the coach with them. They had no idea who she was or why she and the lad had been in the forest with Keir and Eleanor. Little Huey, who'd been soundly sleeping before, now sat wiggling on Colin's lap, asking ques-tion after question and ignoring Fenella's shushing. But Huey's curiosity allowed them to slowly learn one important detail: Mary was Eleanor's long-lost mother. Hannah couldn't help herself. She gave the woman a warm embrace. She could see now the resemblance the woman bore to the painting that had hung for months in Eleanor's room back at Ingledew.

"Start at the beginning. What did you think when Eleanor showed up? Did you know her right away?" Hannah clasped her hands and waited.

Huey repeated the question and Fenella hushed him again.

Mary rubbed her temples and spoke softly. "Aye, I did." She glanced at the boy, Colin, and seemed to hold back some truth she meant to say. She changed the subject. "Who was that man who took her?"

"We doan ken," Fenella said. "But rest assured me brother Keir will stop at naught to retrieve her. Logan, too. They may even reach Castle Caladh afore us."

***

HUBERT DROVE THE carriage, snapping the reins on the backs of the horses, and catching bits and pieces of the conversations inside the carriage. Jack trotted his horse alongside and drew Hubert's attention into a conversation of their own. He talked slightly louder than the sounds of the wheels and the clip-clopping.

"Have ye forgiven Keir fer renouncin' the plan we got ourselves so deep into?"

"Aye, but I'm ashamed of me father," Hubert said. "I kent he was a big part of the plan, offering to train up a Hanover offspring." He repressed a laugh. "Though I think Eleanor dinnae need much learnin'. She has a spark about her."

Jack agreed. "And Hannah too. Logan thinks he can woo her, but I danced with her as much as he did."

Hubert shook his head, a sly smirk on his face. "We'll nay talk of yer mischief wi' the … uh, the ladies. I saw ye dance once with Anabel, too … a *real* bonnie lass."

Jack's face reddened and he pressed his knees tighter against his horse. "Are ye plannin' to leave yer family at Caladh and go after Keir? Or jist leave it to Logan? He shadows Keir whenever he can." He smirked. "I'll get a fairer chance with Hannah while he's away."

"Perhaps." Hubert groaned, "Och, 'tis gettin' darker and I dinnae have a way to light the lanterns."

Jack clucked at his horse and trotted out in front of the team. "I'll lead ye. Me horse kens the way by day or by night."

Inside the carriage Huey played with a pair of round stones Colin offered to him. Mary answered Fenella's last repeated question, "Aye, I havnae seen me dear little Eleanor since she was three. 'Twas a long time ago, fer sure. Do ye ken me daughter?"

"I met her a couple weeks past. She was dressed as a lad at first, but I saw through the ruse." Fenella smiled at Mary. "She's a bonnie lass. I like her."

The carriage hit a particularly deep hole and they all bounced uncomfortably.

32

"Oh," Mary said, "I may be sick again." Her brows narrowed and she looked from Fenella to Hannah to Colin and then to little Huey. "But where's me daughter?"

Fenella exchanged a look with Hannah. "Ye'll see her soon. Ye were knocked unconscious by a lone horse and rider. We best tend to yer injury quickly. We're close to the McKelvey castle."

"Castle?"

"Aye. Castle Caladh. Me sister Rory and me father, the Laird himself, will welcome ye and the lad." She reached across and patted Huey's arm. "And he'll be verra happy to see his grandson, Huey."

Mary put both hands to her temples. "But Eleanor? Is she with Keir?"

"I'm sure she is." Fenella changed the subject, looking at Mary's son. "Nice of ye to let wee Huey play with yer river stones." She stuck her head closer to the window and yelled, "Hubert! Slow down, I almost skelped me heid off the carriage top."

She exchanged a worried look with Hannah. Both women thought Eleanor's mother, Mary, was in grave danger of succumbing to a head injury, same as if she'd been kicked in the head by a horse or mule or fallen against a large rock.

***

LOGAN WANTED TO lose the image of Hannah—*Pascoe*—that kept popping into his mind. Focusing on the lovely Anabel was definitely a way to do that. He'd been so jealous of Keir before when he found out their father and hers had arranged a betrothal between them. Keir was at least five years older than Anabel who was closer in age to Logan, maybe as young as Jack. Keir was adamantly against the union and it looked like Keir was keeping a wall up even now as they stood in the MacLeod kitchen with Will and Alpin and a very nervous looking Anabel.

She, it seemed, was not going to look any of them in the eye, which gave him a better opportunity to watch her. She sliced a loaf of bread into four parts, shoving three of the pieces across the cook's work table at Will, Alpin, and him, and held the fourth out to Keir in a somewhat trembling hand. The chunk of bread, the largest, fell at Keir's feet.

"Oh, how clumsy of me," she said, her voice shrill and, Logan thought, quite embarrassed. "I am not used to doing servant's work. Ye must excuse me."

Keir retrieved it without a word, brushed it off, and bit in.

Anabel disappeared into the larder and reappeared with a hunk of cheese on the end of her knife. She pointed it first at Keir. "Master McKelvey. Ye can crumble off a piece, if ye will." As soon as his fingers touched the corner of the wedge, Logan saw her shiver and she let go of the knife. It clattered to the stone floor, taking most of the cheese still attached.

"Oh, I beg fer yer pardon." Her hair fell across her shoulder and hid her expression from Keir, but Logan, and probably Will and Alpin, could see a look of desperation. "I am meant to be served … like a princess … though I would never run off in such scandalous, outrageous, and shameful a manner as Princess Nora." Logan spotted a tear in her eye. "Such a disgrace."

Keir had already picked up the cheese and placed it on the work table. He used the knife and cut it in four parts. When he handed a piece to Logan, Logan said, "Thank ye, brother. And thank ye, too, Anabel. I hope ye feel better soon. 'Twas a pleasure gettin' to dance with ye at the ball."

Anabel peered at Logan under fluttering lashes. "Ye and yer brother Jack are fine gentlemen. 'Tis good that some McKelveys ken their manners."

Logan's heart went out to her. Didn't Keir see how he'd broken hers?

She put four brass mugs on the counter and spoke to Alpin, "Ye ken where the ale is. Help yerselves." She left the kitchen in a swish of skirts, her head high, and without another word.

Keir chugged down his drink and punched Logan's arm. "Come. We've wasted time, but now we've got help." To Will and Alpin he said, "Are ye good trackers?"

Logan didn't catch the answer as he looked back at where Anabel had stood. In his mind's eye he saw her as she'd looked at the ball: the most beautiful vision of how a young Scottish woman should look. But the memory didn't move him; a different memory intruded. One of Pascoe, dressed as Hannah, posing as the princess … and ruining his fragile heart. What was he to do?

***

CASTLE CALADH APPEARED as a towering giant, twice the size of Ingledew. Hannah peered up at it; even in the dark it was most impressive. She wasn't sure she had the confidence to meet the Laird of

34

such a grand palace and not faint away. A pair of servants carrying two candlesticks each came out to meet the carriage. Hannah could see then that the color had come back to Mary's cheeks. Jack dismounted and Hubert jumped down. The two men assisted the women as they climbed out. Huey and Colin were last. Huey took Colin's hand and raced him into the castle, joyously shouting that he wanted to show him the wooden horse inside.

Fenella took charge, speaking first to the maids. "Elspeth, you ready me sister Elsie's room for Mary. I'll bring her up shortly. Then you can see to mine, which will be best for Hannah," she nodded at Hannah, "and for her friend, Eleanor."

"'Twill be done, ma'am. The Lady Eleanor stayed here before. I'll see to her comfort." Elspeth eyed the small group looking for Eleanor.

"Good. I cannae say when Keir will come with her, but I'm hoping he and Logan will be here by dawn."

Elspeth nodded and handed one of the candles to Fenella.

Hannah looked for some way to help. It was awkward standing here. She could unbridle and unsaddle a horse, or carry a bag, or clean up the steaming, stinking mess Jack's horse just made. She'd been excited to be the princess last night, but her role had always been as a servant before.

Jack, holding the reins of his horse as well as the carriage horses', let out a shrill whistle to wake the stable lad.

Fenella scowled at him. "Really, Jack, why doan ye go wake the poor lad yerself?"

Hannah piped up. "I can hold the horses."

Jack grinned at her. "Nay, princess. Ye mustnae come any closer. Me horse has left a most unsavory present here."

Fenella shushed him and went on with her instructions. "And you, Fiona, please open the guest rooms on the third floor. I'll put me family there. But first ye best take a candle and stand near the barn to help me husband and brother see where to step."

"Yes, ma'am. And the lad that went in with Huey?"

"Aye, I ken where Huey's taken him. That wooden horse is in the nursery still, aye? Ye can make up the maid's bed that's in there for young Colin." She passed her candle to Hannah and took Fiona's second one. "Wait, Fiona, is me father awake still?" She watched Hubert grapple with the luggage as she waited for the maid's response.

35

"Nay, ma'am. 'Tis after midnight."

"All right. I'll speak to him in the mornin'." She smiled at Hannah and Mary. "All right, we have more candles inside. I'll show ye to yer rooms. Hannah, there's a connecting room so when Eleanor comes ye can be at each other's beck and call. And Mary, ye'll nay be far from yer lad."

A girlish shriek, not too loud, came from the entrance. There stood a red-haired woman, with a thinner, younger version of Fenella's freckled face.

"Och," Fenella smiled, "'tis me baby sister Rory. She's a wee bit older than Keir, but soon to be married."

Rory came forward. "Ye ken of me weddin'? Who told ye? Which o' me tattlin' brothers? I wanted to tell ye meself."

Fenella and Rory embraced. Hannah curtsied as Fenella introduced her before everyone headed into the castle. Mary nodded, but still seemed disoriented.

The immense greeting room was as big as the ballroom at Beldorney Hall. Tables lined the walls with vases of fresh flowers. The walls themselves were whitewashed stone painted with red lines to mimic masonry blocks, most rectangles embellished further with hand-painted flowers. Sconces flickered with candlelight and Hannah felt a tangle of excitement—that same mixed feeling of dread and anticipation. This was home to the McKelvey men, two of whom she was having romantic thoughts about even now.

Fenella showed Mary to Elsie's old room, then settled Hannah into a spacious but chilly, suite of rooms. It was well-appointed. There were stacks of books on the mantel, warm knitted throw rugs on the chairs, and a single vase of cattails ready to release their white feather-like innards.

Before Fenella left her alone, she told her that one of the servants would bring Eleanor here should she show up before dawn.

***

LOGAN TOOK THE lantern Keir handed him and led the way, Keir second. Alpin held another lantern with Will following fourth.

"Here's where we last saw tracks." Logan nodded at Keir, holding the lantern down by his boot and well out of his horse's field of vision so as not to spook him. "Ah, there. We missed that they veered off." He raised the lantern and pointed.

From behind Keir, Alpin said, "Aye, 'tis the trail to the kirk, if ye be walkin' and not ridin' in a carriage, but a horse can make it through well enough."

"Best be quiet," Keir hissed. "'Tis after midnight. Any sounds will most likely be the rascal we're huntin'."

They took the trail in single file, Logan first. He held the lantern high when he could, to cast the firelight farther up the path.

"Someone's comin' forth," Logan whispered back to Keir. Then, "Hullo there. Have ye seen a … whoa, what have ye there, man? Is that a woman with ye?"

Keir crowded his gelding up alongside Logan.

A man, hunched over and seemingly fearful of them, cried out, "Jist be on yer way, friends. Here, we'll let ye pass." The man was leading a swayback mare, but he also had hold of a small figure. A child or a woman, Logan thought. The man flung her stumbling to the side and pulled the nag forward. They took several steps into the woods.

The woman, hidden by a small blanket, stopped clutching it and let it slip. The man swore loudly, sounding exactly like a Sassenach.

"'Tis them!" Keir shouted.

"Stay back or I'll shoot her," the man threatened.

The woman—*it must be Eleanor if Keir thinks so*—let out a short squeal and collapsed as if fainting, but in that sudden move she also twisted and brought a long blunt object up hard between the man's legs. The poor man was instantly incapacitated.

He bellowed in pain, but managed to produce a pistol and aimed it not at the tormenting woman, but at Keir. When the pistol failed to fire, he puddled into the ground, the agony of the blow to his privates completely overwhelming him.

Logan felt rather than saw Keir jump off his horse. He dashed past him like a black cloud, heading toward the woman who Logan could clearly see now was indeed Eleanor. She raised the object—a candlestick—to do more damage, this time to her kidnapper's head, but Keir reached for her, and pulled her away.

Alpin and Will had dismounted so Logan did too, quickly tying his horse to the nearest tree and setting the lantern on the ground. The three of them surrounded the man. Logan recognized him then. It was Luxbury, Captain Bernard Luxbury. There was more than a little shouting and swearing from Logan and Keir, and a lot of kicking and hitting from Alpin and Will. Logan's lantern sent flickering shadows across the horses' hooves and onto one Englishman's humiliated and quite battered face.

"Are ye all right, El?" Keir held Eleanor tightly. "Ye'll pay fer this, Luxbury," he threatened.

Will and Alpin pulled the poor man up and tied him to his own horse as Logan pondered the way Keir acted around Eleanor and that he called her El. He'd denied it before, but could she be the lad, El? Or was it a coincidence that the princess had this name? El and Pascoe … the two lads sent from England to help with their plans … wait … he drew in a shuddering breath. Could the reason Pascoe was so good at playing Hannah be that he … *he* … was really a … a *she*?

***

ELSPETH BACK-STEPPED away from Keir as he entered the castle, one brawny arm around Eleanor. The maid stuttered a greeting and told them which rooms the others were in. "I'm to take yer wife up to yer sister's rooms, Master Keir, unless …"

Keir nodded at her. "That'll be fine, Elspeth. And she's nay me wife. Though we'll fix that soon enough."

Elspeth looked down for the few seconds it took for Keir to embrace and kiss Eleanor.

Elspeth took Eleanor up and passed the door to Hannah's adjoining room. "Yer friend'll be sleepin' in there," Elspeth whispered, then walked to the next door, "but ye can get to her room from yers. Here it be." She let Eleanor in and lit a few candles. "I set some night clothes on the bed. Will ye be needin' anythin' else?"

"No."

Eleanor waited until the maid left before creaking open the adjoining door. There was enough light from Hannah's hearth to see the bed and Hannah there sleeping peacefully. She left the door ajar, changed into the sleeping gown, and crawled, quite exhausted, into the soft bed.

***

HANNAH WOKE SUDDENLY to the sound of a dog barking outside. For a moment she forgot where she was, then looked around at the lovely

38

room. The candle had burned down several hours' worth, and early sunlight was peeping under the heavy drapes. The events of the last few days seemed years ago.

She swung her legs over the side and looked around, noticing the adjoining door was now open. Light came from that room, too. Was Eleanor there?

She tiptoed over, looked in, and gasped. The person in the bed sat up and made a similar sound.

"Oh, Hannah." Eleanor held her arms out and Hannah jumped into the bed and squeezed her friend with all the strength she had.

"I was afraid I'd never see you again. It gave me such a scare when you left before the ball." Hannah sat back on her heels, close to the edge of the bed. "But Fenella assured me you'd be safe with Keir. Then that awful Captain Luxbury took off in search of you."

"And he found us, but Laird McKelvey sent his troops back to England and the captain came with Keir and me to look for my mother."

Hannah listened to Eleanor breathlessly tell bits and pieces of the trip: separating from Luxbury, finding her mother, traveling back to Castle Caladh and being abducting by Bernard on the way. "Oh, Hannah, it was awful, but Keir and Logan and two MacLeod men came upon us and rescued me." She shook her head, her face glum, then suddenly she brightened. "Hannah! I know my real name. I saw it on my baptismal paper. My mother had it safely stored all these years."

Hannah blinked repeatedly and focused on Eleanor's face. "And? Your name is …"

"Eleanor Mary Fletcher Hanover."

Hannah's lips formed an O. "So it's true. You're a Hanover. You're royalty."

"There's no proof anymore." Eleanor shook her head. "I threw it in the fire and destroyed it."

Hannah's face fell. "But why?"

"Because Lady Beth warned me to. Without proof that I have royal blood, the insurrectionists cannot use me in their plan. I'm free, Hannah."

Hannah bit her lip and frowned, reading her friend's face. "You don't seem happy about it."

"Well," there was a light knock at the door and then Elspeth, the maid, asked if she could enter, "yes, come in." Eleanor continued, "I would have liked to keep the baptismal certificate, but ..."

Hannah followed Eleanor's eyes to the door. She saw a flash of a McKelvey kilt and her heart jumped.

Elspeth curtsied, tray in hand, and announced, "I've brought ye our cook's special welcoming breakfast."

Both girls slid off the bed and settled themselves at the table before the fireplace. Elspeth arranged the food on the table then tended the fire.

"Mm, bacon." Hannah picked up a piece and sniffed it before taking a bite.

"Be there anythin' else ye need?" Elspeth straightened the bed covers.

"No, thank you, but was that Keir in the hall?" Eleanor asked.

"Yes, ma'am, yer husband ate in his room and said he'll be expectin' ye in the library this mornin'." She curtsied again and started for the door.

Once she was gone Hannah, whose fingers had dropped the bacon at the word husband, asked, "What did she mean? Are you married to that McKelvey? How could that possibly be?"

"Remember how I left the kirk ... kind of sickly? I went to meet Keir. Then we waited in the vicarage until your service ended and all of you, the Beldorney guests, left. We went back to the kirk. It was Keir's plan to marry me so I couldn't be forced to marry the King."

"Oh, I understand. Clever." She lowered her voice to a hush. "So ... are you truly a married woman, El?"

Eleanor sighed. "Not yet. The vicar died before we could pledge our troth." She bowed her head. "And now with proof of my lineage gone, he doesn't need to marry me, but ..." she looked up, a tiny hint of a smile coming to the corners of her mouth, "he still wants to."

Chapter 5

I DOAN KEN who they be. I keep tellin' ye, Rory." Logan huffed and gripped his porridge spoon tighter. His face had gone red with all the storytelling he'd had to do to satisfy his sister.

The smaller dining room held not only those two but also Jack, who added his two pence worth after every statement Logan made.

"I danced wi' the princess," Jack bragged.

"'Twasn't the princess. How many times do I have to repeat it, Jack?" Logan pounded the handle end of the spoon on the wooden table.

Rory looked from one to the other. "Stop yer arguin'. Logan, why do ye say she weren't the princess? Jist who are ye speakin' of?"

"The princess at the ball was … was …" Logan blew out a huff of air. "Och, shite. I might as well tell ye now, Jack. That was a lad. Ye danced with a lad. A lad named Pascoe."

Jack laughed at his brother. "Nay, ye're the one full of shite. I ken it wasn't the real princess, but her companion, Hannah, takin' her place. And Hannah is a right bonnie lass. I met her when we first arrived at Beldorney Hall."

"Nay," Logan glared at Jack, "Hannah is really a lad named Pascoe, play-actin' at a bein' a maid. And I met her—*him*—weeks before that."

Rory laughed and brought a hand to her mouth to cover the grin she was unsuccessful in hiding. "Ye've been fooled, I'm afraid. Fenella would nivver allow a lad and a lass to share her old bedroom suite. And I was talkin' with Keir this mornin', out at the stable, and he's plannin' to wed the lass. And soon, too. On the same day I'm to wed me Rennie. If Keir says they're both lasses, then there's no doubt aboot it."

Her brothers raised their brows, Jack in triumph, Logan in confusion.

Logan set the spoon down. "What do ye mean, Rory?"

"The real princess, Princess Nora, arrived with Keir in the middle of the night. She stayed here before. I lent her me clothes. She's a lass, same as yer three beautiful sisters." She gave them both a sisterly snarl. "So if she's sleepin' in one room and this Pascoe is in the verra next … they're either both lassies or both rather small lads."

Logan rose suddenly. "I doan believe it." He glanced at Jack and just as quickly looked away from his brother's smirk.

***

FENELLA CAME DOWN the stairs as Rory was going up, her younger sister's face redder than usual.

"What's got ye gigglin' under yer breath?"

Rory stopped on the same step and told Fenella about Logan's reaction to learning Hannah wasn't a lad.

"I've been givin' 'im hints and watchin' the fun," Fenella said. "Men are such fools."

"Aye," Rory agreed. "Keir told me aboot all the fuss wi' the captain and the dyin' priest and …" she leaned closer to whisper, "… the boy, Colin. Did ye ken? He isnae Mary's real son, but she's raised him from a bairn."

The sound of a creaking door on the first floor drew their attention. They both looked down.

Fenella whispered, "'Tis father. He's gone into the library. He expects to meet our new guests this mornin', but 'tis a nice day and I'm takin' Huey and the lad, Colin, to the pond. Huey needs a friend. Could ye help Mary get ready and introduce her to the Laird of Castle Caladh? She's feelin' like herself ag'in. No bruises from the knockin' down she got last night."

"Aye, but I couldna help but notice she doesna have much with her. May she be frettin' how to show herself to a laird?"

Fenella scoffed. "Father doesna give a fig what a woman wears or how beautiful she may be. There be plenty of widows would marry 'im, should he raise his eyes to acknowledge one."

"Aye, 'tis true."

"He yet mourns for our mother, but there's somethin' about this Mary. I like her. Could ye take her to me room, the one Eleanor is in, and show her me old wardrobe? Give her anythin' she can fit into."

***

HANNAH WATCHED WITH jealous eyes as Eleanor and her mother embraced. She was glad that her friend finally found her mother, but she felt more alone than she had the stressful hours she was without Eleanor. And it wasn't only that Eleanor had found her mother, but she was going to gain a whole family once she married Keir. Hannah's own future was uncertain. She hoped, but couldn't be sure, that she would stay on as Eleanor's companion or maid or maybe even head housekeeper.

"Hannah, look," Eleanor called out to her as she released her mother, "this is my mother, Mary Fletcher." She caught herself. "I mean, now she's Mary Rose Mcfarlane."

"I know. We brought her back in the carriage. Do you feel better, Mary? You hit your head quite hard."

Mary looked at Hannah. "Aye, Hannah, is it? I'm sorry, I don't remember you."

Eleanor quickly explained their relationship as Rory, who had just brought Mary in, spread several pieces of clothing out on the bed and interrupted to get their attention.

Mary was overwhelmed with the selection and hesitant to borrow a dress, but the four of them had fun deciding what would fit, what needed mending, and what they could wear today. Mary selected a plain light blue frock that though it had a dark stain at the hem, needed no further tailoring to fit.

"What's wrong?" Hannah asked Eleanor as she helped her into a day dress.

"Shh, it's nothing. A little soreness in my arm and ribs from Bernard's rough handling of me."

Hannah huffed angrily. "Captain Luxbury should be hanged and quartered for treating you that way."

"Keir gave him over to the MacLeods who took him away tied to the saddle. He will suffer worse pain in addition to the thrashing I gave him."

"You thrashed him?"

Eleanor whispered so Rory and Mary wouldn't hear. "I caught him hard between the legs with a holy candlestick he stole from a kirk."

Hannah's eyes went wide then she simply smiled, closed-lipped.

"Shall we go down now?" Rory sounded anxious. "Me father is waitin' to meet ye, Mary. Doan let 'im rile ye. He's a bossy man, hard on the outside, but soft as fresh churned butter on the inside."

Hannah looked at Mary's reflection in the dresser mirror. They'd been admiring themselves once they'd changed clothes and now Hannah took a moment more to study her best friend's mother. Mary was so much like Eleanor, not too tall, but with the straight posture of a well-born elite. For an older woman—maybe forty or forty-five?—Mary was not unattractive.

"I've had a bit of experience wi' widowed men," Mary said, "… but not wi' the laird of a castle." She shook her head and amended her statement. "Well, I'll nay blether on aboot it, but there was once a McHenry what had an eye on me."

"Me father's a good man and will treat ye as a guest." Rory smiled and stared openly at Mary. "Can I ask ye a question?" When Mary nodded, she said, "Ye speak like a Scot, but ye're English, aye?"

Eleanor spoke before her mother could. "Folks here aren't always friendly or forgiving of the English … of us Sassenachs. Some folks, I mean. Your family has been most welcoming."

Rory brushed a strand of red hair behind one ear. "Aye, ye're one of us … or ye will be soon. Once ye're wed to Keir, ye'll be a Scot. Now, shall I take ye down?"

That statement made Hannah feel left out, but Rory added, "All of ye," and hooked her arm in Hannah's.

All but Mary giggled on the steps, then quieted as they entered the spacious room next to the library which Rory called her mum's gallery. There were two divans and several carved walnut chairs, a low bench, and massive portraits set against dark paneled walls. Velvet drapes framed two tall windows and the McKelvey crest hung between them.

"This was me mother's favorite room," Rory stated. "When I was a wee lass, I'd stare at the coat of arms and me mother, nursin' Jack in that chair, would tell me and me brothers an' sisters all the meanin's of the symbols and colors."

"It's beautiful." Mary walked closer and stared at the tapestry. "I can guess the lion symbolizes courage."

Rory gave them a brief explanation as they took seats. Hannah kept her eye on the door, hoping a McKelvey man would enter, and trying to decide if she'd prefer it to be Logan or Jack.

"And the helmet denotes wisdom, protection …" Rory's voice trailed off and she looked at Eleanor. "I hope ye ken that Keir—" she stopped mid-sentence as a rather impressive McKelvey strode into the room. At first Hannah thought it was Keir, but the man was older. The Laird of Castle Caladh. She stood up as did the others.

"Guid mornin' to ye, lassies." He gave a somber nod to Eleanor and raised his eyebrows at Hannah and Mary. Rory made introductions. "Verra pleased to meet ye. Ye have a fine daughter, Widow Macfarlane."

"Just Mary, 'tis all I've ever been called." Hannah noted the nervous quiver in Mary's voice and how her cheeks reddened. She looked lovely now.

"Mary, then. Will ye allow me to escort ye aboot the grounds? I saw Fenella take the boys out. I'll show ye a bit of the nature they'll be enjoyin'."

Mary hesitated and Laird McKelvey tipped his head toward Hannah and Eleanor. "And ye lassies must come, too, o' course."

Hannah glanced at Eleanor, ready to go out, but Rory kissed her father on the cheek and said, "I'll show Hannah the castle while Eleanor meets with me favorite brother. I'm sure he wonders why I havnae brought her to him yet." She gave him an affectionate touch on his arm. "Be nice to Mary, father. Doan show her the McKelvey temper if the neighbor's sheep are grazin' on our hills."

"Och," he said, sounding just like Keir or Logan or Jack, "ye may be thinkin' o' yerself. When have ye ever heard me raise me voice?" He laughed loudly over Rory's response and held his arm out to Mary. "M'lady, shall we?"

As soon as they left the room, Rory held a finger up to Hannah, "Jist ye wait a wee bit, Hannah. I need to deliver yer princess here to her intended." She ushered Eleanor out and returned minutes later.

"Well, did ye hanker to see the secret parts of the castle or would ye rather go outside to the ponds and pastures?"

Hannah opened her mouth to speak, but the door flew open and Logan entered.

***

LOGAN GLARED AT Hannah. "Pascoe! Take yer wig off. I demand to see ye as ye really are."

Rory smacked her brother's arm. "Ye can't talk to a lady that way, ye blitherin' idiot."

Logan glared at his sister, his ire rising further. "Ye'll nay boss me aboot, Rory. And ye're guilty of unchristian deception, ye are. What ye said at breakfast … the two o' them, Eleanor and … and Hannah … they're either both lads or both lassies. I aim to learn the truth. If Eleanor's makin' a fool o' Keir …" His face grew hard and he pounded a clenched fist in the palm of his other hand.

"Ah," Rory put her hands on her hips, "'tis yer older brother ye're worried fer and nay yerself. Well, I'll leave ye two to put things aright. Ye'll nay be wantin' me as witness when ye learn how preposterous yer assumption is." She gave Hannah a conspiratorial smile and said, "I'll be in the great hall, near enough to hear yer shoutin' if ye need me." She pushed past her brother and closed the door behind her.

Logan breathed in through his nose, his lips pressed tightly together, as he waited for Hannah to say something.

Hannah put fingers and thumbs to the sides of her head and carefully lifted off the blonde wig she'd borrowed at Beldorney Hall. She placed it on the nearest side table and pulled out the single comb that she'd used to gather her own shorter hair into a clump at the back of her head. She shook out her hair, ran her fingers through it, and said, "There, Logan McKelvey. Are you satisfied?"

His heart thumped an extra beat; he wasn't expecting Pascoe to still look so feminine. "I saw ye, when Tavish brought ye. Ye were wearin' breeches and shirts, the two o' ye. Ye … ye dinnae have such womanly curves." He watched her bosom swell as she breathed. He reasoned that a lad could stuff a dress, but if Hannah was a woman how could she appear as she did that first time, as a scrawny, scruffy lad?

Hannah sighed. "I never meant to deceive you, Logan. Tavish found us on the ship, and he thought we were lads disguised as fine ladies. He

46

threatened to have us thrown overboard so we thought it best to do as he demanded and wear the men's clothes he found." She looked over his shoulder at the closed door. "I suppose you'll learn soon enough ... Eleanor was raised secretly at Ingledew and I along with her. We were accustomed to dressing as boys, binding our chests to flatten them, cutting our hair short ... and our manners ... well, we had few. The Lord and Lady there were neither kind nor welcoming until there was a use for us ... for Eleanor, I mean." She lowered herself into the chair and shook her head. Logan remained standing, arms folded across his chest.

"But what about the lad, El?" He was still confused. "Did he run away?"

"No, that was Eleanor. We had to look and act like boys at Ingledew; I just told you. She was Eldridge; I've always called her El. That's why it was so easy to fool Tavish and you and Keir."

"Well," Logan loosened his arms as she finished, still not sure how he felt, "I'll be athinkin' on this tale fer a while." He turned and walked toward the large family crest and stood there staring up. "If an apology is what ye expect from me—" He stomped one foot lightly, scuffing the edge of a rug and making it buckle.

"No, not at all," Hannah stood up, wiped the wetness from her cheeks. "Logan ... I ... I may never see you again after Eleanor weds Keir. It is I who needs to apologize. I knew you thought I was pretending and I had several chances to confide in you. I'm sorry I didn't."

He turned. Her eyes drew him in and his funny heartbeats returned. He wondered if he could shrink the distance between them and take her in his arms again. This time they wouldn't dance. He would draw her closer than a dancing partner. He could imagine his lips on hers. Already he felt the anger dissipating.

But—

"Do you forgive me?" Hannah bowed her head. When he didn't answer, she gathered the wig and started for the door.

"Pascoe."

"Yes?" She turned and gave him a sad look.

"What does Pascoe mean?"

"It's my name. I'm just an English maid named Hannah Pascoe, from Feock, Cornwall, late of Ingledew Manor."

He took a couple steps toward her and stopped. "And me brother? When did he learn the truth?"

Hannah's complexion reddened. "He spoke to El in the stable, a few nights ago, thinking of course that El was a boy, but it was Eleanor, back in the boys' clothes we had … and … and she told him the truth, but he didn't believe her. He pulled her shirt off … and so ..."

Logan was perplexed. Had his brother gone crazy? First believing El was a lad and then, once the truth came out, wanting to marry her? How could anyone fall that fast?

His eyes were drawn again to Hannah's bosom … there was a fair amount of relief filling his own chest. He opened his mouth, but no words came out. This was good, wasn't it? Since he already did have feelings for Hannah?

"If you've nothing more to say to me, I'll go out to your sister. She was going to show me the grounds and maybe some secret place."

He thought of Rory having left the room only to hover anxiously in the hall, haunting the door like a ghost, waiting. He found his words then. "Hannah! Wait." His chest heaved. He held his hand out toward her. "Set that silly thing down. Ye look beautiful with yer hair as it is." A true smile came easily. When she set the wig on the divan, he tossed a coverlet over it. "Take me hand. I'll show ye a passageway, secret it is, that even Rory hasnae learned of."

***

HANNAH DIPPED HER head as she followed Logan out a hidden door in the paneled room. He had a tight grasp on her hand, but she didn't mind. The warmth of his skin gladdened her. Could it be that all was made right between them? His whole body had lost its rigid tension like when a riled stallion calms when the stable hand calls to it; and his voice had gentled, too

"Won't Rory know about this now when she comes back in and finds us missing?"

"Nay. She'll only think we took the steps beneath the rug … another secret passageway. She'll ken we patched things up and off she'll go to find Fenella." He pulled the panel closed and thrust them into complete darkness.

"Oh!" Hannah had only a glimpse of the small space before the pitch blackness enveloped her. It smelled of wood and mold.

48

"Dinnae fash. I'm pressin' on the hinges." He gave a grunt and light blinked around the edges of another door, lower than the first, that opened onto a fairly well-lit set of winding steps.

"Daylight?" Hannah stepped through and craned her neck.

"Aye. 'Tis a second castle keep, much smaller, with its own tower that rises up beside the first. Me father showed me brothers and me, made us promise to bring our sisters here for safety should there be another uprisin'."

"Why don't your sisters know?"

He shrugged his shoulders. "They cannae keep a secret. Ye ken how lasses are."

Hannah pulled her hand out of his. "So ye still think of me as a lad?"

"Nay," his face puckered, "I think of ye as more than a lass, is all. Ye shined brighter than even Anabel at the ball. Ye could be a true princess. Ye are ... a princess ... to me." He put both his hands on her upper arms. "Pasc—uh, Hannah ... I am sorry."

She saw it in his eyes. It stirred something in her whole being. Was he going to kiss her? Here? At the bottom of a secret staircase? A wave of panic coursed through her body. She remembered a tale from her youth, something about a poor girl kept in a tower like this for such a long time that her hair grew clear to the ground. She raised both hands to her own hair, the movement effectively shifting Logan's hands off her.

"It's my hair. Because it's short you cannot think of me as a lady, can you?" She pulled her fingers through several strands, tugging them downward toward her shoulders.

"Och, yer hair is long enough. Mayhap 'tis the color what misconstrues me thoughts an' words. Neither dark as the maid's nor red as me sisters'. I like it though." He touched a lock and brought his face closer still.

To Hannah it seemed his words spiraled up the tower, somewhat muffled. Her veins rushed blood to every part of her, muting her hearing, warming her middle, yet weakening her knees. This man left her breathless. It was as if he'd cast some fairy's spell that stole the air from her body.

"I ... I can't breathe."

49

Logan gave her some space. "'Tis the air. The damp walls weep wi' lime tears. Can ye climb? 'Twill be better at the top, near the window." He motioned upward. "I'll walk behind ye, in case ye fall."

She lifted her hem, crunched the fabric into a wad she could hold up with one hand, and used the other to press against the stone wall for balance. Up she walked, the steps pebbly under foot, and narrow, her heels never touching. She couldn't imagine coming down; surely she'd fall. But trusting Logan seemed right.

Chapter 6

JACK WAS USED to his older sisters treating him like a baby. He was the youngest, after all, but they refused to see him as a man … which he was … in more ways than one. Perhaps he was spoiled, but in the last year he'd tried to assert himself. He'd learned new skills. He could fight as well as any of the Laird's subjects. He'd proven himself to be a fine horseman. His sword-wielding skills rivaled Logan's though probably not Keir's. Even so, Keir himself had praised his accuracy with the *claidheamh mòr,* the heavy sword passed down from their great-grandfather.

And Jack had mastered the art of dancing as well as the knack for saying what would please a lass or a lady in any social situation. He'd tended his mum more than even his sisters in that last year before she passed. Only to him had she whispered wise words of the heart in regards to love and marriage. Good and special things to know; things his brother Logan probably had no thought of. And now that Logan knew the truth about Hannah, which Jack had never doubted, Jack was ready to put his expertise with the fairer sex on the line against Logan.

"Have ye seen Hannah?" he asked Rory, when he found her pacing outside the library and the portrait room.

"She'll be in there," Rory smirked, "hashin' things out wi' Logan."

"Och, the fool best keep his fingers off her." He pushed open the door, hoping desperately not to see them in a compromising position. He saw no one, but felt Rory's breath at his neck.

"Hah! He's taken her down to the wine cellar." Rory hissed in his ear. "Did ye ken we put Eleanor there when those English soldiers were here?"

Jack didn't answer. He strode to the rug, studied it a moment, then lifted enough to reveal the trap door. There should have been a taut line from the cord used to pull it open or closed, but Jack could tell they hadn't left the room this way. Logan must have taken her through to the secret keep.

"Uh," he dropped the rug back in place, "let 'im guide her 'round the castle. I've got me better ways to impress a lady."

Rory gave him a queer look and said, "I can't believe ye're givin' up so easily, Jack McKelvey. What's got into ye?" She shook her head. "I suppose ye'll sit right here till their heads peep up. It could take all day." She eyed him as he took a seat. "Hm, well, I'll be off to our sister Elsie's."

"Mm," Jack grunted, "ye mean to see yer betrothed what works there, aye?"

"Aye, with everyone here all coupled up, mayhaps ye should ride to the MacLeods'. There's an unwedded maiden there by the name of Anabel. I always thought she'd be a better match fer ye than fer Keir."

Jack folded his arms and ignored her.

***

HANNAH PUT HER face to the lowest peephole and saw the pond; she moved to the next and had a view of the stables. She made her way around the turret looking through each eyehole and surveying the vast lands of the McKelveys'. There was no railing to prevent a fall back into the spiraled stairway, but Logan kept an arm around her waist. She liked it.

"Let me lift ye to that high lookout." Logan turned her to face him, put both arms around her and lifted before she could answer. It meant his face was close to being buried in her bosom as he leaned against the wall, but she didn't mind. She had one hand on his muscled shoulder and the other she set against the wall to protect her face as she peered out.

"We've a larger tower on the southern side, with seats and proper windows, where me mum would keep a lookout for our father while we bairns would play at her feet. I'll take ye there next. What do ye see?"

"I see a horseman going away from here. No, wait, it's a woman. Long red hair."

"A white horse? 'Tis Rory gallopin' off to see Rennie, nay doubt."

"You can put me down now." She put her other hand on his left shoulder. As he loosened his grip on her, she slid down his chest until their faces were even. There it was again: that breathlessness. He'd tightened his hold on her so she stopped sliding lower, her feet still inches from the floor. She squirmed, pressed his shoulders, and squeaked a plea. "Down, please." Her eyes focused on his left ear, then his stubbled chin, his cheek … his lips … then her eyes met his and held there for a very long moment. Was he saying her name or was she imagining it? She could get lost in those very dark eyes. Maybe she already was lost. Hearing things. Her feet touched the floor and she was now looking into Logan's eyes, and maybe into his soul.

With her head tilted upward, their bodies still touching, hearts pounding, Logan's face came closer. Hannah closed her eyes. The soft touch of his lips on hers whipped up her emotions into a maelstrom of confusion and uncertainty. She returned the kiss. Lost herself in it.

"Hannah? Logan!"

Logan held her tighter yet, but lifted his head. She hated that the kiss had ended.

The voice got louder. Someone—was it Jack?—was running up the steps.

She gasped in the stale turret air, blowing it out hot as Logan pulled her to his side and moved her to the farther side of the tower where there was a short bench and no peepholes. He pressed a hushing finger to his lips and left her there.

Hannah, quite weak-kneed, sank onto the bench and listened as Logan started down the steps, hollering to Jack, "Heyo, ye wee pest. Must ye follow me ever'where?"

"We were supposed to be practicin' axe throwin' together. I did it on me own then I was lookin' fer … uh. Why be ye here? Are ye alone?"

"Aye, alone I am. Only spying on our father walkin' the grounds with that lady. And I saw Rory ride off."

"Is Hannah up there with ye?" Jack demanded.

"Nay. Ye ken we can nivver tell this secret to a female." There was a pause; no movement that Hannah could discern.

"Then where is Hannah? That's who I was lookin' fer."

"Is she nay in the library wi' Keir and Eleanor?"

Another pause.

"I dinnae look there."

"Or maybe she's at the pond wi' Fenella and the boys. Was she wearin' brown? I saw a spot o' brown there. Come up and peep out the spy hole fer yerself."

Another pause, then Jack said, "And give ye a chance to beat me there?"

Hannah perceived scuffing on the stones and wondered how anyone could maneuver down the steep and narrow steps so fast. Surely they'd find Jack's bruised and bloodied body at the bottom. She rose from the bench and joined Logan as he came back.

He whispered, "Give him a minute to get out and then we can follow."

She knew what she'd like to do with that minute, but it seemed Logan was now more interested in looking out the highest peephole.

***

LOGAN WAS PLEASED with outsmarting Jack. Now he needed to get Hannah down and out unseen. He ran a hand down the front of his kilt as he peered out the highest spyhole.

"Ye ride, doan ye?" he spoke over his shoulder, smoothed his kilt again and turned.

"You know I do. I sat behind you on that mare you won. Have you forgotten already?"

"Aye. 'Tis a memory I shan't forget, but I thought ye were a lad then."

"Well, lad or lass, I can still ride." She smiled and he melted. "I enjoyed having my arms around you." She blushed and he melted even more.

"'Tis guid to ken. I'd like to do it ag'in, so as to have the feelin' o' yer arms around me middle and kennin' that ye're a she and nay a he."

"One thing, though, 'twould be more proper if I used a side saddle."

"Shall we sneak to the stables then?" Logan grinned at her. "We can ride separately across the heathers and then … when we're outta sight of Caladh … will ye join me on me mare?"

Hannah blushed even deeper. Logan considered repeating the intimate event they'd engaged in before Jack intruded, but his instincts told him to go slower. If there'd been any doubts about her gender, these few minutes in the tower with her had blotted them completely out.

"Come. I'll help ye down. The steps were easier when me feet were smaller." He looked down at her slippers. "Och, ye should be fine. I'll go first though, so ye'll have a cushion should ye slip."

***

HANNAH TOOK A deep breath and set both hands on either side of the curved walls. There'd been small sparks of joy in her dreary existence at Ingledew, mostly having to do with an extra pastry from Cook or the trick of hiding from the stable master's whip. Here at Castle Caladh, though, the sparks were gathering into flames. Logan was the son of a laird, wealthy and prominent, probably well-educated, schooled by his mother, she thought. The lads she knew at Ingledew, the Miller twins and the Chadderton boys, had few prospects. She believed she would most likely someday marry one of them or maybe Cameron, the farmer boy who worked on the neighboring land. The idea of marriage never excited her the way such thoughts now brought about an eager hope.

"Careful," Logan said for the third time. His hand reached up and back, also for the third time, to touch her knee or thigh, whereupon he'd pardon himself for such boldness.

She could have managed well at an even faster pace. She used to climb trees and walk the top of the border wall. She was skilled at balancing, but these steps were certainly steeper than any others, and having Logan right there, so willing to catch her if she slipped … well, she always felt inferior to Eleanor, but at this moment, with no Lady Beth to scold her or stable master to mock her or that dreadful Anabel MacLeod to look down her nose at her … she let the good feeling and a wide smile take over.

And then she slipped.

"I've got you." Logan caught her, scraping one hand against the stones as he scooped her up and leaned them both against one wall.

She got a toe down to touch the step one above Logan's. "Thank you."

They were eye to eye. Nose to nose. And suddenly lip to lip.

***

JACK SEARCHED THE castle, quizzed the servants, and then, on a hunch, headed out to the pond. He made out voices in the stable and turned that way instead.

He found the stable lad holding Copper's reins while Keir attached a bag of provisions onto the saddle.

"Are ye leavin' on a crusade, brother?"

"Of sorts," Keir replied. "I'm off to England to right a wrong and fetch a weddin' gift."

"Fer Rory?" Jack started to grin.

"Nay, though now ye remind me, I'll purchase some bauble that'll please her." Keir finished tying the knot and looked at his youngest brother. "Ye should ken, Jack, that I plan to wed Eleanor the same day as Rory pledges her oath to Rennie."

"That's but three weeks away. I ken by the numbers Rory spouts out each day that passes."

"Aye." Keir mounted the horse and took the reins from the stable lad. "Are ye keen fer an adventure? I'll wait a bit if ye want to gather yer things and some food and join me."

Jack glanced at the next stall where his horse, Soldier, stood. The offer was tempting. He hadn't been to England. The chance to travel with his brother was tempting. There might be confrontations with cantankerous Englishmen, opportunities to wield his sword, join in gambling games, flirt with foreign maidens ... a dozen more possibilities crowded his thoughts.

"Well?" Keir stroked his horse's neck and waved the stable lad off.

"'Tis a long while to be away." He looked up at Keir. "I ... I doan want to slow ye none."

"Och, ye've got yer eye on Eleanor's friend now, doan ye? Ye cannae fool me." Keir gave a hearty laugh and nudged Copper past Jack. "Guid luck, Jack. And 'tis luck ye'll need if Logan means to court her, too."

Jack scowled as Keir rode off. His older brother had guessed rightly about his hesitation to leave. Two weeks away would give Logan too much of an advantage with Hannah's affections. He couldn't shake the

56

recollection of her at the ball, all creamy smooth skin, blushing cheeks, sparkling eyes. He'd had her in hand for several dances. The smiles she gave him … ah … even now they brought his own face out of its scowl.

"What's so funny? Yer face looks like a fairy tickled ye." The stable hand poked the end of a straw at Jack's chin.

He swatted the straw away, resumed the scowl, and went into Soldier's stall.

"I beg yer pardon, sir. Shall I saddle him fer ye? Ye can catch up to yer brother."

Jack shook his head.

The lad persisted. "I was aboot to turn Soldier and the other horses out into the pasture."

"Aye," Jack gave his horse a pat and came out, "ye can do that, laddie." He stopped with his hand still on the stall latch when he heard Logan's voice.

"Ye can take me brother's horse, Hannah. He willna mind."

Jack shooed the lad away, folded his arms, and watched as Logan and Hannah entered the darker space of the stable. He was taken aback for an instant upon seeing her with her hair undone, the blonde locks scandalously short. He cleared his throat. "Which brother would ye be meanin'?" Jack tilted his head. "Copper isna here and I was intendin' to take Soldier for a wee trot along the road to—"

"Jack!" Logan's face blanched and Jack read all kinds of truth in it. "Look, I found Miss Hannah. She was wantin' to see the stables." He avoided Jack's eyes and looked instead at the horses in their stalls. "Father's old geldin' will do ye fine enough." Logan called after the stable boy, "Heyo, laddie, put me mum's old side saddle on Blackie, will ye?"

Jack stepped toward Hannah. It took little effort to make his face return to its previous pleasant expression. The woman before him, though not dressed or groomed in fancy gown and wig, was a vision. The hair that shocked him at first, framed her face like golden lace. And the scent of her somehow masked the odor of stall muck.

"Are ye wantin' to ride out amongst the flowers?" He lowered his voice to a warm rumble, "I ken a place where bluebells grow along the heather. I'll pick ye a bouquet as I often did fer me mother."

Logan took Hannah's hand and raised it a few inches, enough to challenge Jack's offer with the possessive gesture.

Jack's reflex was to grab her other hand.

***

HANNAH REVELED IN the responses she was getting from the McKelvey brothers. On the one hand, there was Logan whose recent attention included devastatingly thrilling kisses, and on the other hand—quite actually—was Jack whose flirtatious enthusiasm enchanted her. His dimpled smile was incredibly seductive. He now held her hand with the utmost tenderness.

"Gentlemen," she said, lowering her eyes and wondering if she should flutter her lashes as she'd seen Anabel do at the ball, "please allow me my hands." She pulled free of them both and stepped toward Soldier's stall. "This looks to be the horse we rode, is it not, Logan?"

"Nay, 'tis Jack's gelding, Soldier. We rode the mare I won from McDoon."

Jack spoke quickly. "If ye'd prefer him, Hannah, I'll take Blackie. Soldier is a good, calm mount. A child could handle him."

Logan eyed him. "A child does, aye."

The brothers glared at each other in the gloomy stable light. Hannah tensed along with them.

"The side saddle is on Blackie," the stable boy said, leading Blackie out of the far stall. "Who should I saddle next?"

"I'll do my own," Logan said, rushing to the wall where the tack was hung.

"And I shall help ye, sweet Hannah," Jack exclaimed, taking her hand again and ushering her to Blackie's left side.

Hannah thanked him, but at the same time gave a smiling nod of her head to Logan who was obviously annoyed with his little brother. As for her feelings, she should have been disappointed by Jack's intrusion, but she experienced another tingle of delight as Jack, just as handsome and strong as Logan, put his hands on her waist to lift her up. Perhaps it was for the best that he come along; she needed a chaperone. And for a moment she wondered which brother … *no, she mustn't have such thoughts.*

Chapter 7

DINNER WAS HELD in the larger dining room. A trestle table was set with places for Laird McKelvey, Mary, Hannah, Eleanor, Colin, Fenella, Huey, Logan, and Jack. Hubert had returned to their farm, Keir was gone on his quest, and Rory had not yet ridden home from her visit to Elsie's.

Hannah, seated between Logan and Jack, kept her blushing under control by turning her attention to Fenella or Eleanor or the Laird as they spoke of Keir, the Beldorneys, the upcoming weddings, or various other topics. Huey drew her attention often as he spouted childish comments, interrupting the grownups.

Hannah had little to offer to the conversations, but nodded and smiled, and observed everyone else. She noticed how quiet Mary was and how often she sneaked longer glances at the Laird. She wondered if there was some special relationship already growing between them, besides being the parents of the prospective bride and groom. Hannah was happy with how accepting the Laird was of Eleanor. She never expected the Scot to allow his son a union with an Englishwoman, and though Eleanor was truly of royal descent, that fact was now to be kept as a family secret. She'd never be referred to as Princess Nora again.

Occasionally, she stopped paying attention to the chatter to think one particular thought: *she mustn't, even for a minute, expect the flirting gestures of the McKelvey brothers to lead to marriage.* She was not of their station. The lad in the stable or the field workers they passed on their horseback ride today were more on her level. She was still play-acting, though no longer as a lad or a princess, but as an equal to Eleanor. She was not her equal, of course; she shouldn't forget that. She was Hannah Pascoe, no pedigree, no parents, no link to royalty or wealth. All she had were the clothes given to her, a borrowed wig, and a smooth, shiny stone Colin had passed to her in the carriage.

"Doan ye agree, Hannah?" someone was asking her.

She glanced to Eleanor, pleading silently with her eyes, and chewing longer.

"I'm sure," Eleanor covered for her, "that Hannah's opinion will be the same as mine. She agrees with you, Fenella, as do I. I will, indeed, wear the tartan colors in my wedding dress, but I'll need help with the sewing."

Hannah nodded her head and swallowed. "I'm afraid such close handiwork is not our best skill. We would do better braiding leather for reins or helping mares foal."

Logan brightened. "Aye, I wouldna ha'e believed it, but Hannah took to riding side saddle this day and did it as well as me mum would."

Jack leaned into Hannah. "Aye, ye did, lass. And with a bonnie expression on yer face."

The Laird spoke solemnly, "Me dear departed wife had a talent with the horses, she did. Do ye ride, Mary?"

The conversation focused on Mary for a while and though Hannah heard Mary's answer at first, the comments that followed were lost on her because Jack pushed his chair closer to hers. His shoulder touched hers and out of the corner of his mouth he whispered, "Will ye ride wi' me at dawn? There's a place where the sun rises and casts twin shadows across our land. 'Tis a sight ye'll nivver see in England, so says the traveling merchant."

Hannah turned her head slightly and whispered, "I'm afraid I won't awaken in time."

"I'll give three taps on yer door."

She turned her head the rest of the way to look him in the face. She intended to give yet another excuse, but the twinkle in his dark green eyes froze her tongue. She nodded her acceptance and heard a sigh, her own.

"Ah!" the Laird startled Hannah, calling out as the dining room door sprang open and Rory burst in, followed by the maid, Elspeth, carrying a set of dishes. "Daughter, ye'll nay stay out so long ag'in. Ridin' in the dark, alone, from Elsie's to here, isna safe, lass."

"I wasna alone." She sat and Elspeth placed a plate and utensils in front of her. "Rennie came along to see me safely home."

"And ye dinnae invite 'im in to sup wi' us?"

"He's still fearful of ye, father."

"I accepted his proposal and am givin' ye a substantial dower." The Laird frowned. "Is there somethin' else I should ken?"

"Nay, father." Rory kept her eyes on her plate and began filling it from the platter Fenella passed down.

Hannah furrowed her brows. She didn't know Rory at all, but she had a peculiar look about her, one she'd seen on a maid at Ingledew ... one who Lady Beth dismissed suddenly when she confessed she was with child.

Hannah stared at her own plate then and promised herself such a problem would not happen to her, however much either of the McKelveys tempted her. And she was definitely tempted. Her body warmed when she thought again of Logan's kisses. And worse, she wondered what it would be like with Jack.

***

JACK BARELY SLEPT all night, afraid he'd sleep past dawn. He kept an eye on the candle, letting it burn down to where he'd marked it. If he was right, he had time to rise, bathe in the pond, and wake Hannah with plenty of time to sneak her out of the castle and ride to the top of the barren hill.

The cold pond water chilled him, but didn't put a damper on his excitement. He dried, dressed, and strode to the stable. The stable lad was snoring like an old man, fast asleep in the last stall. Jack quietly led Soldier out without saddling him. Hannah had insisted yesterday that she could ride bareback, and Logan had boasted that she rode behind him, wearing breeches, and never slipped off. It had annoyed him to think of

Hannah clutching his brother. He was glad though that Logan hadn't realized Hannah was a girl when she'd ridden with him.

He walked Soldier to the castle doors and tied him there. He entered the great hall and slipped up the steps quiet as a spright; he didn't want to wake anyone, but he was especially careful near Logan's door. When he got to Fenella's suite, where Eleanor and Hannah slept in adjoining rooms, he hesitated. He didn't know which of the two Hannah was in, and of course he couldn't go to the third floor to wake Fenella and ask. He took a chance and tapped three times, ever so lightly, on the second door.

He waited. He was about to move to the other door and tap there when the door cracked an inch.

"Jack?"

"Aye, are ye ready?"

The door opened more.

"Yes, but I am looking for a bonnet—"

Jack reached in and took her hand. "Ye doan need one. I like yer hair loose. Ye're the bonniest lass in Scotland, ye ken." He pulled her out and closed the door for her, carefully making sure the latch made no sound.

He kept her hand in his as he led her down the main staircase and out into the bailey. Soldier gave a whinny and pawed the earth as they approached.

"Hush now, ye ole cow, and stand still. 'Tis a lady ye're aboot to have the pleasure of on yer back." He ran a hand down Soldier's neck and patted him. "I'll give ye a leg up. Hold yer skirts high like me sisters do."

Hannah smiled shyly. The horse was tall, but she could grab the end of his mane with one hand and scrunch her skirt up with the other. She lifted her leg and set her foot into Jack's hands.

"Up ye go," he said and let her bounce herself up and onto Soldier's back. He untied the reins and led them through the gate, stopping a few feet beyond. "Take the reins and hold him steady. I need to step upon this rock to get meself up."

He hadn't thought it through. He'd need to grab the mane or else her arm.

"Here," Hannah said. "I've done this a hundred times with Eleanor." She grasped both mane and reins in her right hand and offered her left arm to Jack. They clasped wrist to wrist and she gave him the leverage he needed to heft himself up behind her.

"Aye," he laughed softly in her ear, "ye're a worthy horsewoman, as ye claimed. Did ye ride like this with Logan?"

She tipped her head back to answer and he gulped at the closeness.

"No. I sat behind and wrapped my arms around him." Soldier was starting to move forward and Hannah reined him in. "You can hold on to my shoulders, if you need to."

Jack gulped again. "Nay, I can balance … unless ye urge him to trot."

"I shan't. Which way?"

He pointed then set both hands on either of his thighs. Had he considered it fully, he would have mounted first and pulled her up behind him. It would have been nice having her arms around him; perhaps if they dismounted on the hill they could switch. He'd have to find a mounting rock. At least he was glad he'd pulled on breeches instead of wearing his kilt. He had to wonder how Logan had ridden with her … ah, but Logan thought he was riding with a lad. He smirked and let his lips continue into a satisfying smile.

Ah, her hair smells lovely. A lavender scent.

"Take that path there. Soldier will want to go right, but pull him left. Aye … guid … there ye have it. A fine horsewoman, ye are indeed."

They were on an incline, heading up a hill. Hannah leaned forward and Jack did as well, keeping the same two inches between his chin and her hair.

***

HANNAH WAS CHILLED by the early morning air. She wished she'd brought a shawl … or that Jack would put his arms around her. Could she ask him to? No, that would be too forward. But if he caught her shivering, she would not refuse any warmth he could offer. She wished she was riding behind him. There was some warmth to having his chest behind her back, but it would be so much better to snuggle against him. She closed her eyes a moment and remembered the feeling of riding behind Logan … arms around his middle … chest muscles rippling under her grip … her cheek melting against his back.

The corners of her mouth curled and she breathed out slowly. *Should she be thinking of Logan now?*

She gripped with her legs as the horse started up the hill. She leaned forward and clung to the mane as it grew steeper. Jack's breath never left off ruffling the top of her head.

"Almost there," he said, his two words still in a hushed whisper as if afraid of waking the birds. "Stop him at the peak and face west. We'll have the rising sun at our backs in a wee bit and ye'll be stunned to see the remarkable twin shadows it'll cast."

Hannah glanced around as she followed his instructions. It was still quite dark, the air heavy, electric; they'd be sitting here longer than a 'wee bit' if she knew anything about Scottish mornings in the few weeks she'd been here. But waiting was all right. It was nice to be with someone who wasn't making her work, or teaching her useless manners, or expecting her to—

"What was that?" The sound of—were they crickets?—startled her. Again came three notes of a song shattering the stillness, then a rustling in the grasses.

"'Tis the fairies," Jack teased. "We're blessed wi' them in the Highlands."

Hannah twisted to look back at him. It wasn't so dark that she couldn't see the glint in his eye.

He went on, "Aye, the fairies. They'll be takin' refuge from a change in the weather. I'm sorry I dinnae smell it sooner, but there's rain a'comin'."

Hannah looked up. It was too dark to determine if there were rain clouds above them.

Soldier whinnied. Jack pressed closer and reached around Hannah to stroke the horse. She found it rather intimate that he would do so. She squirmed.

"Are ye cold?" He set his hands on her shoulders and flattened his forearms against her upper arms. "There. Me mum used to warm me in this way when she'd ride behind me, lettin' me manage the reins."

"When was that?" Hannah didn't mind the familiarity.

"When we'd ride to the Highland games. I musta been eight or nine. By ten I could ride alone."

"What are the Highland games?"

"Och, ye'll see at the end of summer. They'll be takin' place at Castle Caladh, they will. Fightin' with swords, throwin' axes, heavin' rocks. The McKelveys won the most last year and so we're hostin'."

There were several moments of silence as Hannah imagined these Scottish contests and Jack gently rubbed up and down her arms, warming her chilled flesh.

Soldier pawed the ground.

"He hasn't the patience to wait for dawn." Hannah chuckled.

"Nay, he's tellin' me somethin'. And by the drops that be fallin' on me arms and head, I think he's warnin' of a storm. We best head back."

Hannah couldn't resist saying, "I didn't believe in double shadows anyway."

"I told ye 'twin' shadows and so ye'd 'ave seen two. Yers an' mine. 'Twas a trick me eldest sister played on me once."

***

THE DOWNPOUR STARTED when they were at the gates. Jack slid off and took the reins, leading Soldier through the bailey and around to the kitchen door where he helped Hannah down and sent her inside.

"Oh, m'lady, ye're soppin' wet." Elspeth came quickly from where she was tending the fire when Hannah entered the kitchen. "What were ye doin' out so early?"

Hannah stuttered some nonsense about wishing to gather night-blooming petals whilst the scent on them was strongest. "But I guess they don't grow in Scotland." She squeezed rainwater from her hair.

"Well, ye jist stand by the hearth and I'll fetch ye some blankets." Elspeth hurried out and Hannah, leaving a wet trail on the stones, moved as close as possible to the fireplace.

She was turning round, front to back, like a piece of meat on a skewer when Elspeth returned with a thin blanket. "Ye can drop yer clothes here," she said, "and wrap yerself up in this. I'll see to dryin' yer things if ye want to return to yer room."

"Thank you." Hannah shimmied out of her wet items and, thankfully, had the blanket completely covering herself when Jack stumbled in.

"Ah," Elspeth hummed, "the young master was also out in this weather." She raised an eyebrow at Jack. "Keep yer eyes averted, young Jack."

He backed up a step, keeping as much floor as possible between them. "I was in the stable, tendin' to me horse. Did ye nay hear the thunder?"

"Well, sir, ye'll be needin' a blanket, too, now." Elspeth gathered Hannah's things in her arms. "'Tis a wee bit awkward to have the two of ye sodden and fer such different reasons. Seems odd ye both were out in the rain before the good Lord brought the start of a new day." She eyed Jack firmly then turned to Hannah. "May I walk ye to yer room, Mistress Hannah?" And to Jack she said, "Ye best stand right there till I return."

Hannah shuffled out with Elspeth who kept giving her sidelong glances without making any accusations. She desperately needed something to say to the maid and finally, halfway up the stairs, settled on, "Have you worked at Castle Caladh long?"

"Barely a year, miss," Elspeth answered. "I came after the Laird's dear wife passed on."

"You seem young."

"Sixteen years this summer."

"Oh," Hannah gave her a closer look, "Eleanor and I aren't much older. Eighteen."

"Same as Jack."

"Are you friends with Jack? I wondered at the way you refer to him … 'young' Jack."

Elspeth clutched the wet items closer as she breathed out an embarrassed denial. "Nay … nay, miss. 'Twould be frowned upon … but … Jack is friendly. He's not like the rest of the McKelveys."

"He's not?" Hannah wondered if she should learn more about Keir, for Eleanor's sake. She was going to willingly marry him in a couple of weeks, but what if Elspeth knew of some questionable personality trait that Hannah should pass on to Eleanor? "What do you mean?"

"'Tis the character of the other McKelveys to be takin' risks. Bold they be. But Jack is sweet."

It didn't bother Hannah to hear that Logan and Keir took risks, she knew that about them, but she wished to learn more. She pulled the blanket tighter around her and took slower steps.

"And Keir … and Logan? What do you think of them?"

"Fine lads, they are. Keir is an honorable man. Logan … he takes after Keir when he's with 'im, but Jack gets him into mischief." Hannah felt the maid's eyes studying her intently. "Methinks 'tis Logan yer heart is after. Ye want to ken if ye can tame him from his mischief or join in, is that it?"

Hannah shook her head emphatically. "Please … please don't tell anyone I was up so early. I know how servants can talk." She stopped at her door and faced the maid. "I'm but a servant myself. Truly. Just a homeless, English maid, at the beck and call of Eleanor. I have no designs on either of the Laird's sons."

"Aye, ye mustn't. I'll tell ye what the cook told me the day I was hired. A dalliance between lord and maid is a pleasure for one and a certain dismissal fer the other." Her voice was low as she looked back at Eleanor's room.

Hannah whispered, too. "I understand. There's no future in a dalliance. But … maid to maid … I'll tell you the truth. Jack took me out on his horse to show me the sun rising. He swore it cast a double … er, a twin shadow if you watched from the hill."

Elspeth put her hand on the door latch and opened it for Hannah who needed both her hands to keep the blanket closed around her. Elspeth chuckled briefly. "Ye aren't the first he tried to trick with that deceit. I'll nay tell a soul, but … ye're destined to be more than a maid, methinks." She curtsied. "Is there anything else ye need, m'lady?"

***

HANNAH DONNED HER night shift and nestled into her bed. She enjoyed a short hour of sleep before Eleanor came in to roust her.

"What happened to your hair?"

Hannah sat up and ran her fingers through the still-damp snarls, but before she could invent a plausible answer—or tell her good friend the truth—Eleanor began naming the things that were planned for the weeks leading up to the wedding.

"I was up so late with Rory … talking. Did you know they've hired craftsmen to come this week and make the benches? They'll be used for the guests at the wedding … weddings … and used again late summer for the Highland games. Did you hear tell about the games?"

Hannah nodded and listened as Eleanor chattered on. Everything was so wonderful for Eleanor. A bright future ahead. A husband. A home. Family. Wealth. There wasn't a jealous bone in Hannah's body, but she did wonder how she'd fit in. What would her future hold for her? The maid's prophetic statement played over and over in her head ... was she destined to be more than a maid? She almost laughed aloud in the middle of Eleanor's explanation of the dress-sewing schedule. Could Elspeth only have meant Hannah could aspire to being something more? Like a companion? Or a nanny to the new couple's inevitable offspring? What other positions were there? Castle seamstress? Shepherdess? Laundress? Cook's helper?

"Pascoe! You're not even listening. Are you all right?" Eleanor put a hand to Hannah's forehead. "You feel fine. Come. I almost forgot. We've got pastries in my room. We'll break our fast and then ... we have to do something about your hair."

Hannah made a silent promise to herself to pay better attention to her friend and to help all she could in the wedding preparations.

Chapter 8

HANNAH KEPT QUIET about her secret meetings with either Logan or Jack in the weeks that followed. She flitted between helping Rory and Eleanor with their wedding preparations, but when she could, she'd sneak off with one or the other of the McKelveys, to ride through the woods or walk the fields or explore the castle. Those times, though brief and secret, filled her with longing. If only she wasn't a mere maid; if only she had some royal connection or elite parentage. She'd felt herself falling more for one of the brothers, but since she had no hope of a future with either, she continued to divide her attentions between them. She was disappointed that Jack had not yet tried to kiss her and equally disappointed that Logan seemed to pull back. There'd been no repeat of the delicious kisses in the secret turret.

Finally, the day of the weddings arrived. Hannah gathered with Rory and Eleanor, and Mary and the McKelvey sisters in Rory's spacious bedroom. There was no need for a fire in the hearth on this warm morning. Helping the brides get ready involved last minute dress alterations for Rory as her mid-section was thicker than the week before. The sisters blamed Cook's fancy tarts, Mary suggested it was monthly bloating, but Hannah and Eleanor exchanged knowing glances.

Hannah felt a twinge of jealousy when Eleanor hugged Rory and expressed her gratitude in sharing the special day with her. Hannah let out a sigh and stepped to the window. Guests were arriving.

"Oh, my," she said, "look at all the carriages."

The ladies stepped closer then went back to fixing dresses and fussing with hair. Hannah and Mary worked on weaving flowers through Eleanor's hair while Elsie and Fenella did the same to Rory's red locks. Their fingers took on the flowery scents and got smudged with pollen. Every few minutes Hannah or one of the others went to the window to see how the crowd of guests was growing. It was quite noisy, then a hush came over the people and the sounds of the hired piper floated up to them.

"How nice," Hannah said. "I wonder what that tune is."

"We ken it," Fenella said and the three McKelvey sisters sang the Gaelic words as Mary finished with the flower petals and Hannah bent to tie Eleanor's shoes.

"'Tis too tight," Rory suddenly exclaimed. Fenella sang another line of the song as she loosened the laces on Rory's bodice.

Hannah stepped to the window once more to see if she could see Logan or Jack among the guests, but there was no sign of them. She turned back to see mother and daughter whispering to each other. She couldn't deny being happy for her friend. To have found her mother was certainly something to celebrate. She barely remembered her own mother.

The singing stopped and the piper's tune was a bit more solemn, though the high notes of the flute seemed happy. It perked up Hannah's ears.

"Isn't that lovely?" Eleanor said.

"It makes me think of fairies," Hannah answered, moving over to touch Eleanor's hair again.

"Oh," Elsie clapped her hands, "'tis the stone-passin' tune."

"Stone passing?" Hannah looked up from straightening the wreath-like crown of purple heather on Eleanor's head.

Rory turned, careful not to disturb her own laurel of rare white heather. "'Tis an auld custom. The folks below are givin' their good wishes and blessin's onto the stones. We'll place our hands on them when we say our vows."

Hannah sighed again. She was losing her dearest friend. Would they still see each other daily? Would they share secrets and have adventures like before? She suspected the answer must be no. She swallowed the bittersweet thought and declared Eleanor ready. She stepped back to admire the bride.

"You are both beautiful brides," Mary pronounced with a wide smile.

"We should go down now," Fenella said. "I hear the first drones of the bag-pipes warming up."

***

LOGAN SAW THE look in Keir's eye. He and Jack were in for a scolding.

"Och," Keir growled, "ye'll nay be thinkin' of yer tricks."

Logan glanced at Jack whose face scrunched into a scowl. "But we kept the McDoons from comin' and doin' the blackenin' on ye. Ye must let us do the shootin'."

The blackening was an old custom of covering brides and grooms in treacle, soot, and flour to ward off evil spirits. Logan didn't mind skipping that. He was more interested in firing off his newest pistol.

"Ye'll nay do it durin' the vows." Keir ordered. "Ye'll give me bride a fright. The English ways are different. Eleanor dinnae ken aboot the feet washin' or the blackenin' of the bride and groom. Though she'll see it when comes yer turn."

"The piper stopped," Logan gave Keir a rather hard cuff on the arm. "The evil spirits are chased away. Ye'll have guid luck now, brother."

Keir huffed. "'Tis luck, to be sure, to find a woman like El, to love her and have her love ye back. Ye two should be so lucky."

Logan squinted at Jack. He'd seen Hannah in the north pasture picking flowers with Jack yesterday. He didn't like it. Jack glared back at him.

Keir nodded to the other group of men: Rennie, Elsie's husband, and another friend. They nodded back, ready to make their entrance behind the first bag-piper. Rennie stepped forward, his groomsmen on either side of him, and started walking behind the musician up through the guests. The McKelveys watched.

Also watching from the side was Laird Finley McKelvey. He strode over to his sons and embraced Keir, patted him heartily on the back without a word, then went into the castle. He reemerged a moment later

71

with his daughters. The married girls went first while Rory clung to her father's arm, but kept her eyes fixed on Rennie, now standing under a floral canopy.

Once the first wedding party was settled in their places, Keir said, "'Tis our turn, lads." He took a deep breath and touched the plaid draped over his left shoulder. Logan and Jack fell in behind a second bag-piper and Keir followed. They marched between the benches and took their places under the arch.

Logan elbowed himself slightly in front of Jack. He smiled over at his sisters and noted how beautiful Rory looked. There was nothing bonnier than a Scottish lass on her wedding day.

He glanced at Keir whose face changed before his eyes. The poor senseless dolt seemed mesmerized. Logan looked where Keir was staring and saw the second bride and her maids walking forth, Eleanor on his father's arm. Eleanor certainly looked as bonnie as Rory, but his gaze got stuck on Hannah. His jaw clenched and his hands balled into fists. There was moisture forming in his eyes and he could not control it. What was the matter with him?

The ceremony seemed brief, but no wonder, he'd been in a trance much like a dream the entire time. When his sisters broke the wedding cakes over the brides' heads, he came to and gripped the pistol he'd tucked under the band of his kilt. Jack beat him to the first shot over their heads.

***

JACK SHOT FIRST and watched the ladies jump, then there was laughter and revelry as a few more men shot once or twice, just enough to mark the occasion as a completed event. Several women rushed the brides to collect good luck pieces of the cake. Jack aimed the pistol down and looked at Hannah who was smiling with eyes closed and her palms over her ears. Beyond her he saw Keir sweep his bride up into his arms and skirt the crowd. Logan nudged him and pointed, laughing.

"There goes a happy man," Logan yelled over the din as the couple disappeared into the castle.

"Aye, and happier he'll be by night's end," Jack answered. "Step aside, brother, I promised to escort Hannah to the feast." He enjoyed the glare Logan gave him. "Ye should offer yer arm to McDoon's sister; she's been eyin' ye since she arrived."

"Nay, 'tis only her effort to make ye jealous. The lass is closer in age to ye."

Jack recognized how controlled Logan was being, but he knew how to provoke his brother. "Aye, the same age as Hannah, ye ken. And since I already promised Hannah I'd sit with 'er, ye best offer yer arm to Megan McDoon and come sit with us young'uns."

Logan's teeth clenched, the muscles in his jaw quivered, and he jerked his head to the right. His expression withered. "Och, McDoon himself is walkin' off with Hannah."

Jack's head swiveled and he quickly said, "Aye, so he is. And off I go to take yer advice. Megan McDoon is a bonnie lass."

***

LOGAN CONGRATULATED HIMSELF for not slipping into his old ways. As the middle brother, he tried to act more responsibly like Keir, but his younger brother often prompted him into rash and rambunctious behaviors. His recent time spent mostly with Keir had given him some perspective. A year ago he would have tussled physically with Jack, ignoring manners and public decorum in favor of getting his way. And his way today was to spend time openly with Hannah, in front of his father the Laird, and all their guests.

He raised his chin and let a lungful of air out his nose. He had backed off in his intentions toward Hannah, afraid to repeat those glorious moments when he had her in his arms and kissed her. Afraid they'd go too far. The lasses of his land-owning class were schooled in keeping the proper distance from lads like him, waiting for the arranged marriages rather than running off with someone of their own choosing. Hannah was different. She'd accepted his rather rash advance, even enjoyed it, he was sure.

He glanced around as the guests, his father and sisters, started heading toward the tables set up in the gardens. Several servants were lifting the benches and moving them there. He watched Rory and Rennie take their seats at the head table, followed by his other sisters and their husbands. It occurred to him then that all three, as well as Keir, had ignored the custom of arranged marriages and chosen their mates. Why couldn't he?

He could. And he was going to make his choice obvious. Right now. Dylan McDoon was as fickle as a butterfly. He wanted Anabel MacLeod when she was betrothed to Keir and now he must have divined Jack's interest in Hannah. Well, if he thought he could govern Hannah's attention today, he was going to be surprised by this McKelvey.

***

HANNAH TOOK THE arm of the young man who offered it. She knew who he was and assumed he'd been assigned to her by Fenella. Fenella had overseen so many details of Rory's wedding—and Eleanor's—that pre-paring someone to escort Hannah to an appropriate seat seemed kind and thoughtful. She never expected to be included as much as she was.

"I'm Dylan McDoon, m'lady. I've come to yer aid. 'Twill be me pleasure to see ye to yer place and serve ye as I'm able."

She assessed the man quickly: auburn hair, reddish beard, a nicely muscled arm, measured strides she could keep up with. And a deep voice.

"I am pleased to meet you, Dylan. Are you the McDoon who lost a race to Logan?"

"Och," he slowed their walking, "ye ken of that bit of nonsense? Why, I dinnae have the fairies' luck wi' me that day. Lost me favorite mare."

Hannah smiled. "And I've ridden her. But Logan doesn't know her name. Can you tell me?"

"Aye, we called her —"

"Dylan!" Logan pushed between them. Hannah dropped her grip on Dylan's arm and moved aside. Her heart started pounding; she felt trapped and keenly alive. "Mistress Hannah. I'm so thankful that me friend here, Dylan McDoon, has led ye this far. Dylan, me friend, I'll see the lady to her seat. She'll sit wi' the McKelveys. And there'll be an extra seat there, should ye wish to join us." He leaned into Hannah, took her hand and placed it on his arm, and whispered, "We need to fill the table as Keir has fled the celebration with his bride."

"Oh." Hannah looked toward the castle, her eyes rising to the windows on the second floor. "I saw three servants take trays of food and wine into Keir's room. Is this another custom, like the cake and the shooting?" Dylan had moved to her other side and was hinting at offering his arm again. She had feared there might be a confrontation between Logan and Jack, but not Logan and this McDoon fellow. Her heart hammered.

74

Dylan laughed. "Keir kent what was in store. He's locked himself and his bride in their room. Ye'll see though. We'll be separatin' the other bride and groom as soon as they've supped. The women'll take Rory to her room and strip her bare and lay her on the weddin' sheets. We men'll do the same to Rennie and carry him up to her."

Hannah felt her face grow hot.

Dylan touched her hand again, grinning. Why was this Scot so insistent? The only thing she could think to do was set her other hand atop the one she had on Logan's arm, signaling that her full attention was on Logan.

"Ye've embarrassed the lady," Logan spoke across Hannah and dropped his elbow which pulled her closer.

Hannah's eyes darted around the gardens. Most guests had taken their seats. She saw Jack sitting with a pretty young woman. Should she be upset that his attentions had found a new focus? No, in fact, she'd felt more pangs of jealousy over Eleanor. She forced herself to smile up at Logan.

"I'm fine, Logan. I'm not disconcerted in the least. But I am hungry. We were so busy getting ready I barely ate a thing today."

Chapter 9

DYLAN MCDOON OPENED his eyes and peered at the McKelvey crest on the wall above him. It took him a moment to remember where he was. Ah yes, the weddings. He and his brother had come in his parents' place in their carriage ... and with his sister, Megan. He closed his eyes again and wondered if they had taken rooms at Caladh ... no, he remembered now ... his brother threatened to make him walk home. He must have made good on the threat and driven Megan home in their carriage.

Shite! That meant he was without a horse even. How drunk had he been? Exceedingly drunk, he realized, for here he was stretched out on a floor rug, his kilt unpinned and spread over him like a blanket, and his backside somewhat exposed if he were to judge by the cool air snapping at his bare skin.

He sat up and immediately lay back down. His head pounded. The McKelveys' ale was well-aged, indeed.

There was a timid knock on the door. Dylan covered himself completely as the door gently opened.

A comely maid stood there with a tray. "Beg yer pardon, Master McDoon. I've gathered fer ye some of Cook's pastries to break yer fast." She took tentative steps across the room and set the tray on an end table.

Dylan squinted at her. "Were all the bedrooms taken?" He leaned on an elbow, but kept a hand on his kilt to hold it down. There was a breeze attacking him from somewhere.

"Nay, sir. Ye could 'a taken rest on the third floor, but ye complained o' how the steps kept movin' and I couldna bear ye up."

"Hmph. What is this room?" He turned his head to the tapestry and the McKelvey crest.

She poured something from the pitcher into a stein. "'Twas the Laird's mistress's favorite room, I'm told. A place to read and meditate."

"I see nary a book." There was no way he could reach the food until she left. He needed to roll himself into his kilt before he could rise.

"There are books a plenty in the library. Next door." She curtsied. "Will ye be wantin' anythin' else?"

"Nay, ye can go." She made it to the door before he asked, "Are the young McKelveys, Logan or Jack, awake?"

"Nay, sir. They're still in their rooms, m'lord, since they left ye last night wi' the last pitcher of ale."

Dylan grimaced and let her words tumble around his head; there was a subtle scolding in her manner, he thought, but not enough to reprimand her since she was not a McDoon servant. He stared after her until she closed the door. He breathed in and out a few times and stood up. Should she come back in now, she'd get a shocking eyeful. That would cause a passel of tongue-wagging amongst the staff, but not enough to outrage a McKelvey—if they even learned of it.

He laid the kilt out on his belt and set the pleats, then rolled into it, pinned it, and stood. He spotted his boots by the fireplace and put them on before grabbing the largest pastry, apple-filled and still warm.

He needed a way home; he wouldn't even consider walking, not with this headache. He should take back the horse he lost in that bet with Logan. *An donas dubh!* He should have won that race.

He downed all of the cider she'd poured and headed for the door. He swung it open only to step back quickly as he came face to face with Hannah.

"Oh, I'm sorry, I didn't know anyone was in here." She started to turn.

"Dinnae go. Have ye eaten yet? There are pastries there." He swished his hand and bowed enough to cause his hair to tumble onto his forehead and an ache pierce his skull.

"I have. I was … I was looking for a place to … uh … I don't know. I feel rather let down with the end of all the festivities."

He motioned her forward and she inched into the room.

There was something about her. He'd felt it yesterday when he took her arm and then, when he sat across from her at the wedding feast, he found himself studying her face.

"Ye're from England, aye?" He completely ignored his hangover.

"Yes, I was raised with Eleanor at Ingledew. I'm … I'm but a lady's companion, not a lady myself."

"Ye shallnae be treated as anythin' less. By me honor." Dylan swept his hand toward the cushioned seats and led her to one facing the crest. Once she sat, he took the chair opposite. "I saw how Logan treats ye. Am I wrong to think there's a prospective, uh, alliance there?"

"Oh, no, no, there cannot be. I'm … I'm a nobody."

He reached for the tray and offered her a pastry as he smoothly shook his head and said, "The McKelveys wed whom they wish. The Laird allowed his daughters, Elsie and Rory, to shun his selections and marry farmers. Did ye ken?" He did not wait for Hannah's response, but went on, "And Fenella's man, though well-bred, a Beldorney he is, was intended fer another. I'd lay a wager on Logan choosin' ye … but …" he held back a smirk as an idea came to mind, "if ye'd like to hurry things along … I may be of service."

Hannah bit into the roll she'd accepted and cocked her head as she chewed.

"Are ye up fer an adventure? I ken ye ride. I'd like to take me old mare out on the lane. Surely Logan wouldnae mind. Would ye come wi' me?" He puckered his face into a childish plea.

***

HANNAH WONDERED IF she should find someone first to ask about letting their guest use a horse. A grudging shiver of suspicion ran up her middle, but she ignored it. What would the harm be? Certainly Dylan was a friend of Logan's, a friend who would treat the horse—and her—with the care and courtesy of a friend.

"I do like to ride … and I have nothing else to do." She touched the strings to her bonnet, especially glad she'd put it on before leaving her room.

Dylan crinkled his eyes as he held out the last pastry. When she declined, he said, "All right then. Shall we go?"

He held an arm out and she took it, thinking how easy it was to be a lady. Her practice as such, and also at the ball, gave her a bit more confidence. She remembered now how Dylan McDoon had approached her at the ball, intent on having a dance with the mysterious princess, but Jack had cut in front of him and later she'd noticed him dancing with Anabel MacLeod. She wondered now if Dylan recognized her from that night or if the intervening weeks had dulled his memory. She wondered …

"Ah," he said as they entered the great hall, "there's the wee maid, come to fetch the tray."

Hannah smiled at Elspeth and was about to tell her where they were going, but Dylan said, "If the young McKelvey, er, the middle one, has need of his horse, please tell him Mistress Hannah is giving the mare some exercise. And … I'll be takin' good care of me hen."

"Yes, m'lord." Elspeth curtsied and hurried past them.

At the stable Dylan ordered the stable boy to saddle two horses, then frowned and held a hand up to stop the lad's movement. He looked at Hannah and asked, "If ye're truly up for an adventure, we could ride bareback …" he lifted his eyebrows "together."

Hannah glanced at the stable boy whose expression was neither surprised nor judgmental. She supposed he'd seen Rory ride that way many times. The Scots weren't nearly as reserved as the English.

"All right." She let her lips turn up in a smile, but again, something pricked her conscience.

"Get a stool, me lad." Dylan sounded excited. "And I'll lead Toaty out."

"Toaty?" Hannah furrowed her brow. "Did you name her after a toad?"

"Nay, toaty means small or tiny." He brought the mare out of the stall, grabbed a bridle from a hook, and slipped it on the horse. "She was a wee thing when she foaled. We dinnae think she'd survive. But she grew and grew. I was a fool to bet McKelvey and lose me Toaty to him, but I was sure she could beat his nag." He scanned the stalls. "Boy, where's Logan's other horse? The one with the white stripe down its face?"

The stable boy appeared, a crude wooden step in hand, and answered Dylan as he set the step beside the mare. "Out tuh pasture, m'lord. Will this step do? I havnae got a stool."

Dylan gave a disapproving grunt and held his hand out to help Hannah. She mounted easily, her skirts flaring over the horse's rump. She reached back and gathered them, tucking them as well as she could under her own rump and thighs. Dylan stepped up and Hannah surprised him by grasping his arm and pulling.

He landed well. "Och, I see ye've ridden double before. I dinnae ken that women … of yer class … er, uh, …" He left the thought unfinished and she knew why. Though a ward of Lord and Lady Edgeworth of Ingledew, she was not high-born.

Hannah reined the mare out of the barn and into the bright morning light, made brighter by the furious singing of crossbills and nuthatches. They started toward the path she'd been on with Jack. When she got to the fork, she turned right to avoid going up the hill.

"I left me pistol in the castle, but I think we'll be safe enough from the riffraff that Laird McKelvey allows to inhabit their lands."

She felt Dylan's breath on her neck, but it didn't thrill her. In fact, it made her feel nervous. It was one thing to play the brothers off each other, innocently, as it was at first, but it was quite another to flirt and now interact so personally with Logan's friend. She knew what she had to say.

"Dylan … I'm sorry I didn't get a chance to dance with you at the Beldorneys' ball."

"I'm sorry, too," he said in her ear. "I wasn't aware that you attended. What color did you wear?"

"I … I was the one in the princess's gown. Did you not know?" She felt him tense up behind her. She reined Toaty to a halt and twisted around to speak to him. "Eleanor went missing and I took her place so as not to embarrass the Baron and Baroness. Truly, you did not recognize me?"

He breathed out a nay and something about the purple veil. She smelled sour apples on his breath. She turned to face forward. "Perhaps we should go back."

Without warning he grabbed around her, took the reins, and yelled a command at Toaty. The horse began to walk. Hannah had the foresight to lean forward and grab a clump of Toaty's mane. Dylan squeezed Hannah, pinning her arms down, but she still had hold of the mane and a firm leg grip on the horse, though that tended to make Toaty move into a trot, and then a canter. Before she knew it, they were off the trail and onto a cart path.

"Ahh," Dylan grumbled into her hair, "ye've got good balance." He pulled back on the reins and slowed the horse. "Ho, Toaty." Once stopped, he slipped down, pulled off Hannah's left shoe, and looked up at her. "There now. Ye're at me mercy, wench. Ye'll stay astride me horse as we walk a ways. I havnae thought it through, but I'm bettin' ag'in and this time I'll win. If ye're the real princess then Logan'll want ye back enough to trade ye fer me Toaty."

"But I'm not the princess. I just told you. I took Eleanor's place at the ball … and why did you take my shoe?"

"So ye'll stay on me mare and nay try to jump off an' run."

The shivers she'd ignored multiplied and ran the length of her body, down to her toes.

"Why … why would I run?" She glanced back at the way they'd come. It would be a difficult path to maneuver unshod. She used both hands to grip Toaty's mane.

Dylan's handsome face morphed into something evil as he stared up at her. He took one of the reins and wrapped it around her wrists and knotted it. "There. Ye're at me mercy now, ye trollop."

***

"THEY'VE GONE?" LOGAN frowned at Elspeth.

"Aye, sir, 'tis past nuin. Ye're the last to awaken. The new brides and grooms 'ave left the castle."

"I kent that Rory and Rennie were going to move into the wee cottage at Branaugh, but are ye sayin' Keir has left too?" He ran his tongue over his teeth. He could still taste the tang of fermented cider.

"Aye, he had a carriage waitin' on 'em at nuin. He's takin' his bride on a trip to England and France." She smiled and curtsied.

81

"Well, is Fenella still here?"

"Nay, they and all the other guests broke their fasts and left."

"So it's only me and Jack and me father." He let a low groan slip from his lips.

"Aye, and the bride's mother, Mrs. Mcfarlane, and her boy. The castle is quiet. The Laird has given us the rest of this day to rest, but if ye need somethin' I can surely help ye."

Logan scratched his chin and started stumbling toward the kitchen. He turned suddenly and looked at Elspeth. "And Pasc—er, uh, Hannah? Where might she be?"

"Oh," she gave a nervous curtsy, "I'm sorry, Master Logan, I fergot to tell ye. She went out with the young McDoon, the one what spent the night on the floor under the tapestry."

That bit of news brought him out of his groggy stance. "McDoon!" He swore and then apologized to Elspeth. "Do ye ken where they went? To the gardens? The pond?" He walked past her, heading for the door, but listening for her response.

"Nay, sir, he said to tell ye that Mistress Hannah was going to give yer mare some exercise. And he also said … oh, I beg yer pardon, sir, I don't remember the whole message. Somethin' aboot a chicken or a hen."

Logan's eyes went wide and he muttered more curses under his breath. He felt the maid's eyes on him as he hurried to the main doors. He barely heard her griping words, complaining of the improprieties of ill-bred ladies and gentlemen who weren't as mannerly as they should be. Logan knew exactly what she meant. Dylan McDoon had a male-volent side. He'd been pricked by Dylan's sword too many times to believe the mishaps in their sword play were always accidental.

"Where's me horse?" he yelled out the moment he entered the barn. All the stalls were empty and the lad was nowhere to be seen. He went out and ran down the path to the pasture. Far out he could see the lad among eight of the castle's steeds, leading two of them back.

He stood fuming, hands on his hips, as the boy approached. As soon as he was within earshot, he yelled, "Get the racing mare."

The boy looked confused and hollered back, "The Laird has need of these … to pull the wagon."

82

Logan knew right away what he meant. His father intended to take Eleanor's mother to see the ruins of the Strathnaver castle. They'd spoken of it at the wedding celebration.

Logan ran toward them, took hold of the halters, and urged the boy to run back for the mare. He cursed the delay and ground his teeth. It couldn't be anything good if Dylan was off somewhere secluded with Hannah. He hitched the horses up rather than wait idly, then ran into the stable to retrieve his saddle and reins. Out in the field the stable lad caught the mare with the stripe down her face. Logan counted the remaining animals. The number didn't make sense. If the newly married couples had taken two mounts each, whether to ride or to pull coaches, and here stood the pair he'd hitched, and if Hannah took the mare he'd won from Dylan … He counted again. There should be one less than there was, for Dylan came by coach … he'd have had to borrow another horse to ride alongside Hannah.

Unless …

He growled again. That McDoon was such a dobber. He rushed into the stable again and counted saddles.

***

HANNAH GLANCED AT the sky often as they journeyed on. She had an approximate idea of where Castle Caladh was and she was fairly certain that either Dylan was going in circles on purpose or he was lost. They went from meadow to woods, down paths, and up hills that would better be called knolls or hillocks. The beauty of Scotland was lost on her though she was aware of the woodsy scent of the forest they now entered.

Dylan stopped suddenly and scowled at her. "I need to take care of a wee bit o' business. I order ye to stay still." He waved her shoe at her, hostility in his eyes.

Hannah gave the slightest of nods, but as soon as Dylan tied the other rein to a branch and walked a good ways away and then behind some bushes, she slipped off the mare's back and used her teeth to work the knot loose on the strap that bound her wrists. She knew she had a minute or less to hide herself. If there'd been a stump to stand on, she would have remounted and raced off, but Dylan had spoken twice on their trek, and once was to warn her that Toaty was trained to his whistle and would return to him in an instant, should she contemplate escape.

Where could she hide?

She looked at the tree Toaty was tied to and made her decision. There were several sturdy branches, the first within easy reach. She gathered her skirts and scrunched them upwards until she had a wad she could tuck under her chin. If Dylan saw her like this, he'd get an unseemly and uncouth eyeful, but this was her best choice. There'd been a time in her youth, when she and Eleanor had dressed as lads, played as lads, and even climbed trees as lads, and now she was going to have to use those childhood skills to escape this horrid young Scotsman.

She put her bare foot up first, pulled with her hands, and pressed with her thigh. Up another branch, blindly going by feel as her head stayed down. Six feet up, ten, fifteen. Until she was high enough. She lifted her head and let her skirts waft down. Lucky, she thought, that the outer garment was a mossy shade of green. She had an arm around the trunk and both feet, one bare, one with a shoe, on a thick branch. As long as he didn't look up and she didn't dislodge any more needles and no sounds left her lips … maybe, maybe she'd get away with it.

She waited. How long did it take for a man to empty his bladder? A minute? She was certain more like five or six minutes had passed. She didn't move. Beneath her, Toaty's ears flicked forward. The animal must have sensed him coming.

A whistle pierced the air.

The horse pulled on the single rein that tied her. A flurry of brown needles fluttered down from the action.

A Gaelic curse echoed through the woods.

Hannah knew Dylan had seen the horse was riderless. She kept her eyes looking down on Toaty.

Saw him grab the loose rein.

Heard him swear again. Watched him scan north, east, south, west, north again.

Saw him throw her other shoe to the ground.

He swore in English and jerked at the tied rein, tugging rather than untying, and thereby causing another rain of tree debris.

Don't look up. Don't look up.

He brushed the brown gunk from his hair, ripped the rein free, and leaped up on the mare's back. Two seconds later she saw nothing but ground in that space below her. Her ears worked hard to listen for the direction and speed he was going. She counted to a hundred before lowering herself to sit upon the high branch. Her heart still pounded, but her head told her she was safe.

As long as she stayed where she was.

She could do that.

She once hid in the Ingledew pantry an entire night to avoid the butler's punishing rage.

Chapter 10

JACK SAW LOGAN race off on the back of the mare that was the fastest of all they owned. Jack bit his lip and smiled inwardly. He was on his way to the pond for a quick dip, more sure now that he'd have a chance to meet quietly and secretly with Hannah. With Logan galloping off alone, he reckoned he'd have the rest of the afternoon undisturbed.

"What are ye doin'?" It was the boy, Colin, who startled him, coming out from behind the stone statue. He glanced about for Colin's mother, Mary.

"I'm headed fer the wee loch, to bathe meself."

Colin frowned. "But ye bathed afore the weddin's. Why do ye need to bathe ag'in so soon?" Colin came toward the center of the bailey.

Jack laughed. "Och, ye'll learn soon enough. If a man wants to court a lady, he must keep the stink away. A lady's nose bein' more sensitive than a man's."

Colin's frown deepened. "The Laird is courtin' me mother, aye? Are ye challengin' 'im?"

An even louder laugh bubbled up from Jack's belly. "Do ye think me old enough? I'm the youngest of the McKelveys. Not yit nineteen."

Colin's face relaxed. "I'll be thirteen winter next."

"Man enough, then. Come along and have a swim."

The boy fell in step beside Jack, withdrew a couple of stones from a pocket, and began to toss them alternately into the air, catching and tossing again.

"How long have ye been sittin' alone out here?" Jack tried to make conversation with him. The boy had been obscured by the statue, but must have seen Logan race by.

"Long enough to see me mum and the Laird stroll to the barn and then up the hill." He dropped a stone and quickly picked it up. "And afore that, me new sister's friend, uh …"

"Hannah?"

"Aye, Hannah. She went with that fella who drank too much and couldnae walk the stairs last night."

Jack touched Colin's arm and stopped. "Hannah went with … was it Dylan McDoon? Where did they go?"

"I doan ken his name. They rode off on a mare … together … sittin' close … without a saddle."

It was all clear to Jack then why Logan had raced off. It crossed his mind that perhaps he should be jealous, but though he liked Hannah, she wasn't on his mind this morning. He had enjoyed competing with Logan for her, but he wasn't getting anywhere with her and if he was going to lose out to Logan or even to Dylan … well, there'd be plenty of other lasses coming to Caladh for the Highland games.

Colin dropped a stone and bent to pick it up. "Did yer brother hope to save her from a ravagin'?"

"A ravagin'? Dylan wouldn't lay a finger on her."

"Ye think I'm too young to ken such things, but I can spot a fella who's bent on pokin' a lass wi'out her permission." He tossed one stone higher yet.

Jack stopped walking and snatched the stone. He stared at Colin. "Pokin'?"

"Aye. Me mum worked wi' me at the cotton mill. 'Twas a long walk we'd take to get there. Worked three nights a week. We'd pass hoor houses comin' and goin'. I learnt plenty about it. Seen the blokes who'd spend their wage on them hoors. Me mum kept her hair under a cap and dressed like me … two lads we were … and we'd run past them places."

"Are ye sayin' Dylan stole Hannah away for … for immoral purposes?"

Colin held his hand out and Jack dropped the stone in it, waiting.

"Aye. He had the look."

***

LOGAN WAS NOT thinking clearly, he realized. It was impulsive to race off, weaponless, in a direction he wasn't sure was the way to go. He slowed the horse and looked for tracks. The thoughts that swam before his eyes alternated between undesirable possibilities: Hannah falling off and breaking bones, getting lost and wandering hopelessly, or being attacked by highwaymen. He imagined highwaymen holding her and Dylan at gunpoint and discovering they had no coins on them … it was unthinkable that Hannah might be kidnapped … or worse.

Then memories of the more pleasant moments they'd spent together the last two weeks came to mind and riled him more.

"Easy, Blaze," Logan cooed, settling the horse with a couple of long strokes down its neck. The animal picked up on Logan's emotions. "We're going to find her. She'll be all right." He patted the horse again, this time trying to calm his own nervous fears. "Dylan's jist bein' a peacock, struttin' fer the lady, and showin' off."

But what if Dylan wasn't just stealing back the horse he'd lost to Logan in that bet? What if he was taking the mare and the lass all the way to the McDoons'? He raised his head and looked around. He needed to retrace his path and find the trail that led northeast.

Blaze had an easy trot, more comfortable than other horses. Logan might have enjoyed the afternoon ride in any other circumstance, but his skin was prickling with anxiety. He wasn't aware of any sounds except Blaze's snorts and his own grumbled oaths.

When he did hear a far-off shout, he reined in Blaze and listened. Was that his name someone was shouting? He turned the horse around and rode back up the last ridge. He spotted a horse and rider in the valley and waved in acknowledgment.

"Have ye seen McDoon?" Logan asked as soon as Jack reached him. Jack shook his head.

"What are ye doin' followin' me?"

"The lad, Colin, saw McDoon ride off clutchin' Hannah. He thinks McDoon has spite and malice on his mind."

"Aye. The maid delivered a message from that scoundrel McDoon and there was a wee threat in his words. 'Tis why I'm followin' their tracks."

"Which way should we go? Should we split up?"

"Nay. I'm happy to have ye trail after me fer once. Did ye bring a sword, a pistol?"

"Nay, I dinnae even think to wear me dirk since I was aimin' to take a dip in the pond."

"Och," Logan groaned, "we've naught but our fists. When I find that Dylan McDoon, I'll introduce him to both o' them."

***

AFTER THIRTY MINUTES in the tree, Hannah carefully descended, stopping to look and listen every two feet. When she reached the ground, she slipped on her other shoe Dylan had dropped. Her first dilemma was deciding which direction to go. Twigs cracked and snapped under foot as she headed toward higher ground. She was fairly sure the castle lay a mile or two in the direction the sun was headed. It might take till sundown to walk that far, but now that the panic had subsided and she had a plan, her natural optimism kicked in. The only things she might fear now were snakes.

And people.

She heard the voices and instantly ducked, making herself as small as she could. Their scent reached her nose. She recognized the stench of unwashed peasants. Hunters, they were. And not very good ones either, alerting every living thing and failing to see her crouching behind a bush too small to hide her completely. Again, the green dress was a fortuitous choice.

The words faded and she rose to hurry away in the direction they'd come from. A quarter mile later she sniffed the air and recognized that same body odor along with a hint of campfire smoke. She'd found the hunters' cabin. There was woman spreading wet breeches and shirts on a tree limb to dry. A small child clung to her hem. She scooped him up and went into the cabin, unlacing her bodice as she went. Hannah assumed she'd be busy nursing the child for a while. Should she steal the men's clothing? She'd be better able to run in breeches than the cumbersome green dress. And if Dylan should happen upon her, he might ignore her immediately.

She pulled off her bonnet and started stripping her clothes off. When she walked away wearing the damp shirt and breeches, she looked back at the clothing she'd left. She hoped the poor woman would appreciate them, but if not, there was enough material there to make two sets of men's things to replace what she stole.

She squeezed the ends of the shirt and dripped the brown water into one hand. She dampened her blond locks and finger-combed them flat against her head. She lengthened her strides and pretended she was walking alongside Eleanor. So many times growing up they had fooled numerous people into believing they were English stable hands, cursing and tussling and picking their noses. They copied slouching postures and humorless expressions and punched each other like the boys they knew did.

She bent to touch the ground, dirtying her fingers and fingernails, and then smudging a bit on her forehead. No one would recognize her as a lady now.

Well, maybe Logan would.

She walked faster, now on a wider cart path, and thought about Logan McKelvey.

***

DYLAN MCDOON WAS not a stranger to predicaments, none of the McDoons were. His brothers and half-brothers were, at times, surly pests to their neighbors. They were notorious brawlers, but also respected huntsmen and smart negotiators. Dylan could be charming or conniving, compassionate or callous, depending on mood or situation. He did, however, have certain honorable traits: he paid up on all bets and was loyal to his clan.

He never intended to steal back Toaty. The idea of riding with Hannah was ill-conceived, based on a desire to return home. He thought he'd enjoy her company, and once on McDoon soil, he could saddle up one of his horses and ride back to Castle Caladh, returning both Hannah and horse.

But then … something the woman said clouded his thinking, irked him so much he irrationally reacted, calling her names and turning his mood into an angry fit. No one understood him when he got like this. His sisters hated him; his father punished him more than the others; and his unexpected outbursts made their servants tremble and shake.

90

He had, however, learned how to pivot, lying to protect himself, using sweet words in fake apologies, or blaming others for his actions. He had tied Hannah's wrists, taken her shoe, and led her and the horse along various paths, thinking, calming himself, trying to come up with a solution to his impulsive conduct.

Should he laugh it off and apologize? Sell her to a whore house? Take her somewhere and leave her? Ruin her? Let her go? He left her for a short while, just long enough to relieve himself and to think up a believable excuse for his behavior. He thought he had a solution and walked back to her. But … only Toaty was there, still tied up. The girl was gone.

An donas dubh!

He'd get more than a slap on the ear from a McKelvey for letting the girl go missing.

He couldn't take Toaty back and say he rode alone; the stable lad knew the truth.

He couldn't take Toaty home, he had to return her to Castle Caladh. But … if Hannah got there first … before he could charm himself into her good graces … shite, he had to find her. A clan war would be the worst thing.

He circled back, calling her name gently, but lost his way in the forest. He came out onto a cart path and trotted along that way for a while, shouting every now and then. He passed farms and then saw two riders in the distance. Perhaps they'd seen her. He urged Toaty into a faster trot and then a canter. A wave of adrenaline coursed through his body when he recognized Jack and Logan.

Quick, he had to think up what he needed to say before he reached them. He pulled his face into a frown of worry. Acted nervous and concerned. Anxious. Upset.

"Hey-o!" Logan yelled first, pulling up on his horse, and stuttering out his questions. "Where's Hannah? What'd ye do with 'er?"

"Calm yerself," Dylan tried for a contrite smile. "We had a bit of a disagreement … she wished to walk a while." He twisted at the waist and looked back down the trail. "She's jist a ways off. Doin' lady things, ye ken. Ye have sisters. I'm givin' her a wee pit of privicy, I am."

Logan relaxed only momentarily before Jack piped up with, "Ye were ridin' bareback on yer mare and—"

"Not *me* mare. 'Tis Logan's now. I honor me wagers. 'Twas Hannah's choice to ride her as she's familiar with Toaty here." He looked squarely at Logan. "We were bringin' her back to ye when … she needed the jakes … and as there be but bushes and trees …" He tilted his head, gave a friendly smile, and raised his eyebrows.

Logan cast an eye toward Jack. "Stay wi' this rascal. I'll look fer Hannah." He slapped his horse's rump and took off down the lane.

"She'll be along soon, if yer brother doesnae spook 'er." Dylan resumed his smile, shrugged his shoulders, and ran his hand up and down Toaty's neck. He belched and laughed. "Mayhap she should ride wi' one o' ye. Me breath may put her off."

Jack merely scowled at Dylan then looked up the road and waited.

Chapter 11

A M I REALLY and truly lost?" Hannah said aloud. Her skin was itching from the wet clothes. She'd changed directions twice already and still hadn't met anyone on cart path, road, or trail. Scotland, at least in these parts, was scarcely populated. It wasn't like at Ingledew, which she was beginning to long for, where neighbors were plentiful and one could always hear a coach rumbling along nearby or far off.

The sun was in her face and she decided to keep walking toward it as long as she could. But when she came to a creek, she stopped. There'd been no water-crossing on Toaty, so at least she realized she needed to stay on this side of the water. She walked along the water's edge for a while before acknowledging her thirst and scooping up a handful for a drink.

A bit further she came upon a bothan and remembered the one that, weeks ago, she and Eleanor had used to change into dresses. The small hut's door was open and inside, dark as it was, she found a sleeping pallet and a single blanket, crusted with mold, but serviceable. She was tempted to lie down for a moment. She'd been walking for hours, it seemed, and in these worthless shoes.

She shook the blanket and then took the stick that leaned in the corner and propped it against the door, effectively locking out any other traveler. She took off the wet clothes and laid them over the angled stick to dry, wrapped herself in the smelly blanket, and lay down.

Just an hour, she told herself. Time enough to dry the things and rest her limbs. She hadn't noticed before, but she'd scraped her leg and both arms on the bark of the tree she climbed. She sighed and closed her eyes. Just for an hour. No more than that.

***

LOGAN CAME GALLOPING back to Jack and Dylan.

"She's nowhere to be found," he yelled at Dylan. "Show us where ye last saw her." He caused his horse to spin in small circles as he waited for Dylan to take the lead.

"She can't have gone far," Jack said, urging his mount into a matching gait behind his brother.

With a clenched jaw and lips so tight they paled, Logan kept alongside Dylan. A quarter of a mile later, Dylan pulled up and glanced around.

"It was right here," he lied. "Och, women, they be such trouble."

"And the trouble will be yers, McDoon, if we doan find her soon." He stretched an arm out in the opposite direction. "Ye keep searchin' yonder. I'll keep to this side of the heathers, up to the wee burn where the waters run fast. Jack, ye best take the lane to Caladh. If either of ye find her, take her to the castle. I'll nay go back till morn."

He didn't wait to see if his orders were obeyed; he knew they would be. The urge to hurry translated into Logan putting pressure against Blaze's ribs. The horse reacted, ready to run wherever his master directed, but Logan confused the beast by reining him in.

"Easy, Blaze." He inadvertently made the horse back up and turn. In doing so, he looked up to see Jack on the right path homeward, but Dylan was angling off in the direction of the McDoon lands. No matter, the dobber was useless anyway. He'd deal with him once he got Hannah home safely.

He reined Blaze in the direction he meant for Dylan to search. He'd get to the stream, if need be, when it got dark and the sound of running water would guide him.

94

"Hannah!" He began his shouting and stopped to listen every hundred yards or so. His eyes were sharp, maybe not as far-sighted as his sister Fenella's eyes were, but he could spot an owl in a tree, a rabbit in the grass, or a fawn in a thicket. If Hannah was out here somewhere and made the slightest movement, Logan was sure he'd see it. His hearing was sensitive as well, but there was much to disregard. He had to eliminate the sounds of a rodent on crunchy leaves, the buzz of industrious bees, a bullfrog or bird or …

What was that? He heard a different vibration. A clank and then a thud.

"Hannah?"

***

LOGAN DISCOVERED TWO hunters carrying the game they'd taken down, a half mile further on his search.

"Have ye seen a lass? Alone, she'd be … an' wearin' a bonnet, I believe, and dressed as well as a lady." He tipped his head in greeting though he'd spoken none.

"Nay," the older of the two said, "we've been huntin' all day and havenae seen a soul, nor much game." He held up two scrawny rabbits.

The other man squinted at Logan and said, "I recognize ye. Ye're a McKelvey, aye? I watched ye and yer brothers at last year's Highland games. Ye won the caber toss and the hammer throw."

Logan grunted "Aye," though it was Keir who'd won those events. Logan had come in second, but won the sheaf toss by a yard. "Do ye ken where a lass might take shelter? Are there bothans aboot?"

The older man looked to his companion and frowned. The other said, "There be one by the stream." He lifted the hand that held the rabbits by their unlucky feet and pointed with his whole arm. "A long walk, but as ye're on yer horse, mm, maybe ye'd get there by dark."

"I thank ye." Logan spurred his horse in the direction indicated.

The other man called after him. "Er … ye might take the path through the woods first and ask at the widow Douglas's cabin. She kens things ye wouldna think a person could ken withou' the help o' spirits." He snorted as if to scoff at his own conclusion.

Logan gave a nod and headed for the woods. He knew of the widow and her reputation. No one doubted her sincerity or her religious faith. Had she been accused of witchcraft or evil doings then she'd have been burned or banned long ago. But Widow Douglas was a good woman, rightly dividing scripture, and—most important to him—spoken highly of by his own dear, departed mum.

"Hey-o," he hollered when he came out of the woods and was within sight of an old cabin sitting in the middle of cleared land. When there was no answering greeting, he dismounted and checked the dwelling. The door was propped open, a stewing pot on the fire inside, fresh bread on the table, but no one around.

He walked around the outside and noticed a walking path along the edge of the property, disappearing down a hill. He followed it and was surprised to find a small loch at the base of the hill and an old woman wet up to her knees, dipping a bucket in the water.

"Guid evenin'," Logan called out. "Widow Douglas?"

The woman turned, her long white hair tied back with a ribbon and hanging in ringlets down her back. A nearly toothless smile brightened her face. The wrinkles there were deepest on her forehead.

"Aye. Who be ye?" She put a hand to shield her eyes from the setting sun. "Nay, let me chance a conjecture … with the sun framin' ye from behind, yer shape reminds me of Laird Finley McKelvey. Be ye one o' his sons?"

"The second son, Logan, I am." He stepped forward and reached for her bucket. "I'll carry that fer ye."

He also held his other arm out to help her up the hill. She clung onto him with such fragility that he wondered how she would have carried the bucket all that way.

"Will ye join me fer a supper? It's been too long since I've had company to share a meal and spin a tale."

"I'd like to, Widow Douglas, but I'm searchin' fer … fer someone missin' … me, uh, a lady … an English maiden. Some men … hunters … told me ye might ken her whereaboots."

"Missin'? Lost? Or runnin' away?"

Logan's jaw clenched. "Abandoned. She was ridin' wi' the McDoon lad and he let her … uh, he left her to have a bit of privicy … and then he … he couldna find her ag'in."

They reached the cabin and went inside. Logan set the bucket down where she pointed and the widow said, "Ye can sit there, in me dear Ewan's chair. Gone he's been these last six years."

Logan sat. "I'm sorry … but … do ye think ye can tell me where the lass may be? Her name is Hannah."

She put a dipper in the bucket and filled two mugs, set one down in front of Logan, and drank from the other. "Well, I'll need to pray on it a wee bit." She closed her eyes briefly while holding the mug to her chest.

Logan watched her face change as the wrinkles relaxed and her eyelids fluttered. A moment later they popped open. She set the mug down and got two bowls then used the same ladle to scoop out the stew she had simmering. "We'll eat first and I'll keep an ear out for the good Lord's answer to me question."

The aroma of the stew suddenly hit Logan's nostrils and his mouth began watering. "Thank ye."

***

JACK REACHED THE castle at the same time as his father, Laird McKelvey, returned from showing Mary Mcfarlane the Strathnaver ruins.

"We've a most dire circumstance," Jack said, looking from his father to Mary. "Hannah is missing. That rascal, Dylan McDoon, stole his horse back, with her on it, and rode off." He waved an arm southward. "He left her out there … somewhere … lost and alone. Logan is still searchin'. That McDoon …" He refrained from cursing in front of Mary.

"The poor lass." Mary's brow furrowed as she turned toward the Laird. "Ye must gather some men, Finley, and go lookin' fer the poor thing. She's been a sister to me daughter. Any number of horrible things could befall 'er."

The Laird nodded his head. "Aye, I'll see ye safely inside first, Mary." He took her arm. "And Jack, sound the alarm and gather the men. Have Laddie get me horse saddled."

***

LOGAN GREW IMPATIENT. He barely tasted the fine stew, cooling it on the spoon and gulping it down in a hurry. But the widow was not to be rushed. She dipped her bread in, dribbled the juice back into the bowl, then sopped up more, savoring each mouthful and speaking favorably after each swallow. She spoke of memories she had: Highland games her husband had excelled in before Logan was born; the sad deaths of loved ones including his mother; the weather this spring and the outlook for

97

her farmland which the good Laird of Castle Caladh always sent men to, to plant and weed and harvest.

"I thank ye much for this dinner, ma'am, but the sun has set and I best keep lookin' fer me, er, fer Mistress Hannah."

She reached across the table, took his hands in her bent and withered hands, and prayed. He listened, keenly aware of the warmth in those hands, the feeling of peace that came over him, and the Gaelic words that were interspersed among the fervent pleas she made.

"Amen."

"Amen."

He watched her face. Her head nodded as if agreeing with some unseen, unheard answer. She opened her eyes and smiled.

"Ye'll find her." She let go of his hands and rose. "Best ye water yer horse first. Take him to the loch and then follow the trail along the shore. When ye come to the woods ag'in, let yer beast have its head. He'll choose the right way."

If it weren't for the bit of assurance he'd felt during the prayer, he would have dismissed her directions as nonsense and superstition. Surely, he shouldn't leave the finding of Hannah up to a horse's inclination … an inclination that would undoubtedly lead him back to the stable on McKelvey soil. But he did have that moment of faith. He thanked the widow, left a coin on her doorstep after she'd closed it, and rode down the path on Blaze.

The horse drank its fill and they headed into the darker woods.

***

HANNAH'S NAP STRETCHED well beyond the hour she intended. She awoke with a grumbling in her middle and it wasn't for lack of food. She was ill. She never should have drunk the water in the creek.

The bothan was dark inside, too dark to see, but she was certain the door was where her feet were pointing. She rose and stepped carefully, groping with her hands until she felt the now dry clothing. She grasped the stick she'd laid them on and pulled. The stick and the clothes dropped to the dirt and the door swung open. She lurched through the opening and barely made it outside before she began to retch.

There she stood, nearly naked, bent at the waist, gagging and puking at her feet. When she finished, she looked up at the black sky. There were few stars and no moon. She'd never find her way to the castle in this blackness. Her only choice was to reenter the bothan, get dressed, bolt the door as before, and wait until daylight.

She spat on the ground a few more times. The hoot of an owl startled her and she rushed back inside. Once she had the shirt and breeches on, she felt safer. Her lower middle began to rumble then and she feared she'd have to rush out again eventually, but for now she wrapped herself in the stinky blanket and lay back down.

Would anybody even miss her?

Hannah slept more deeply after the purging and didn't waken at the first sounds of someone testing the door.

"Hullo. Anyone in there?"

The voice, unfamiliar, brought her out of her grogginess in an instant. She bolted upright, her heart suddenly racing. Light-headed. Breathless.

"Anyone in there?" Lantern light breached the cracks in the front wall.

She cleared her throat, lowered the timbre of her voice to the deepest bass notes she could produce, and answered in what she hoped was a Scottish brogue, "Aye. Ye wakedme frommeslumber." She spoke too fast, needed to slow it down. "Be off with ye. Let a tired man sleep." She finished with a rumble at the back of her throat as if clearing away a load of mucus.

The man outside spoke to someone else. Hannah clutched the blanket up to her face. She made out a couple words. Whoever they were, they decided to move on. She loosened her grip on the wool. She had no idea there'd be a demand for shelter so late in the day, well past dark. She should have been prepared for the possibility. *Breathe in ... breathe out. I wish Eleanor was here.*

Something crawled past her leg. A mouse looking for crumbs? It didn't faze her. Had it been a snake, she might have screamed and alerted the travelers outside to her gender, but a mouse wasn't worth getting upset over. She slapped a hand down and sensed it scurrying away, out whatever gap in the bothan's frame was closest.

What if they come back? Her skin still tingled and now she needed to relieve herself.

She rose from the pallet and felt her way to the door, checked the stick that wedged it shut, and ran her fingers across the door, feeling for a gap large enough and high enough to peer through. When she found one, she pressed her eye up to it and tried to discern the figures walking away. It was useless. Too dark. The sway of lantern light only produced eerie moving shadows. She pressed an ear to the opening and listened. Grumbled words. Disappointment. Saddles creaking. Horses snorting. Someone coughing. Hoofbeats, slow and fading.

She let her breath out. Looked again. The lantern sparked, then disappeared.

How long should she wait before opening the door? She really had to go.

***

BLAZE PAWED THE earth and nickered when Logan stopped him as they came out of the forest and onto a cart path that went north and south.

"I'll trust yer horse instincts." Logan loosened the reins expecting Blaze to turn left toward the McKelvey lands, but he didn't. "Ah."

He caught a glimpse of swaying light ahead, coming his way. Once again, he lamented the fact he had no weapon with him. There were two horsemen and the lantern light glinted off at least one sword.

"Hey-o" he called, "friend or foe?"

There was no answer at first, but he could determine the men were leaning close, conferring. Blaze whinnied again and the approaching horses answered.

Logan saw lamplight glint off swords, there were two, now liberated from their sheaths and held ready.

"Friends of the good Laird McKelvey," came the delayed response.

Logan's lips parted and he looked heavenward for an instant. "Aye, and glad I am that ye be our friends." He was close enough now to discern the faces. "Dougal … Robert … can ye spare a moment to help me?"

Dougal answered, "Ah, 'tis Logan. What help do ye need?" He sheathed his sword.

"I'm lookin' fer Hannah Pascoe, a young English maiden, good friend of Keir's bride, lost hereaboot this day."

"Aye, we ken. Yer father, the Laird, has us and ten others out searchin' the roads, the hills, the woods."

Logan should have realized. There'd been time enough for Jack to get to Caladh and beg their father to sound the alarm.

"No luck, I see."

"Nay," Robert answered. "We went all the way to the creek." He pointed back with his sword. "Woke a traveler barred up in a bothan there. But nay sign of a woman anywhere."

"Barred up, ye say?"

"Aye. Strange it was. Must have wedged the door with a log." Robert fumbled with his sheath, his other hand challenged with reins and lantern.

"There's nay reason for such defense ... unless he was protectin' a woman. Or it was a woman." He looked beyond them. "Are ye sure 'twas a man in the bothan?"

Dougal looked at Robert and they both shrugged. "Sounded like a man."

Logan didn't resist the sixth sense he felt. "Show me where the bothan is."

Chapter 12

HANNAH FINISHED HER personal business and stared up at the night sky. A cloud passed and a few stars glittered above her. She grimaced and shivered. Quenching her thirst was a priority, but drinking from the nearby creek was unthinkable … unless she could boil the water. Mightn't the bothan have a pot and she just didn't see it? She took careful steps toward the hut. Her mouth seemed so dry she couldn't cluck her tongue.

A pot. Looking for a pot.

How could she start a fire?

Flint?

Might there be flint left inside for a weary traveler?

So thirsty.

She stopped walking and closed her eyes tightly. She thought back to the day, not that long ago, when she and Eleanor stepped into a different bothan to change from rags to dresses. They'd held back their giggles knowing they were going to get quite the reactions from the men with them, Logan and Keir and Hubert and Thomas. Cross-eyed Thomas had been staying in the bothan. She remembered now the scent of ashes, pine sap, and rabbit stew. So perhaps this bothan would have … what? … something …

Uf, was there a tremor underfoot? Her head ached. She felt rather dizzy; she might need to puke again.

With a mix of hope and dread she picked her way back to the front of the structure. She left the door open, not because she thought there'd be enough delicate starlight to penetrate inside, but because she thought … she thought … what did she think? … oh, yes, it was better open in case she needed to run out.

She knew the pallet was to the right … she went left, feeling up and down along the rough walls. Her toe touched something hard. How had she missed this before? There was a small hearth. The faint odor of ash reached her nose. She ran her hand along cold, hard stones, knelt down to grope and then …

A noise outside.

She froze, one hand on a stone the other on the dirt floor. The air moved around her and she had a sudden sense of falling. There was cold dirt against her face. *What?* She'd been squatting and now she was lying on the ground.

Creak of leather, heavy breaths … horses? … men?

They came back! A stingy rush of adrenaline cleared her head. Could she rise and close the door in time?

Someone called her name; her heart jumped to her throat. She stumbled out and into the lanternfall. Stopped short and gasped.

"See?" A voice said. "'Tis only a boy. Where's the man with ye, lad?" A blurred figure balanced a lantern on his knee; the angle sent light to the face of the man on his right. Logan.

Thank goodness, it's Logan. Her hand went to her heart and then she dropped to her knees, unable to utter a single word before she dry-heaved.

***

"OCH," LOGAN SHOOK his head, "ye're right, Dougal, 'tis a lad. Here, hold me horse. And ye, Robert, see to the lad. He'll well need yer water gourd. I'll look in the hut."

He strode past Hannah without looking down at her. He inspected the bothan inside and out. Some of the walls had crumbled in places, revealing dark rotting wood.

The ominous-looking sky seemed to reflect his mood as he walked back toward Dougal and Blaze.

Robert rose from tending Hannah, the empty gourd in his hand, and took a few steps away. "He's beyond peely wally, Master Logan. Might it be a plague?"

Logan shuddered. "Gi' me the lantern, Dougal. If the lad has a rash …" He shook his head and grasped the leather handle, swung the lantern out in front of himself to light the way, and heaved a sigh at this delay in searching for Hannah.

"Show me yer face and neck, lad." He bent close as Hannah, wobbling on hands and knees, tipped her head back, looked him in the eyes, and groaned.

Robert chuckled. "Sounds like a dog, he does."

Logan knew instantly. He slammed the bottom of the lantern into the dirt and scooped her up, then ordered Robert to bring the light into the hut. He carried her inside and set her carefully on the pallet.

"Hannah, Hannah, can ye hear me? What be wrong wi' ye, lass?"

Robert grunted as he set the lantern down near her head. "Have ye gone daft, Master Logan? 'Tis a lad."

Logan ignored the statement. "Bring me Dougal's water gourd then both o' ye ride to Caladh like the wind. Bring me back wine and blankets and fresh well water. And Cook, too. Have her pack the herbs she uses when one of us is sick."

Robert frowned, but obeyed.

"'Tis half empty," Robert said as he returned and handed Logan the second gourd.

Logan unstoppered it and put one hand under Hannah's head to raise it. "Here, Hannah, sip slowly." The edge of the gourd's rim touched her lips. She sipped and a dribble trailed down her chin. "Ye needn't watch me nurse her, Robert. Go. Make haste."

"'Tis a lad, sir."

"Go!"

***

HANNAH KEPT SIPPING, eyes closed. She might be dreaming, but she didn't care. This dream included strong arms around her shoulders, cool lips on her forehead, soft words in her ear, and most importantly, water on her tongue.

"Stay still. Ye have a fever."

"Mm?"

"Hannah. Ye're ill. I've sent fer help. Here. Drink a wee bit more."

"Logan …" she murmured.

She drifted in and out of consciousness. The next time she opened her eyes there was daylight streaming in through the door. Light that hurt her eyes. She squeezed them tightly closed.

And voices. So many voices. Men. Logan. A woman. Familiar … not Elspeth … not Eleanor … of course not Eleanor. It was the cook. It was the Castle Caladh cook … not the cook from Ingledew who came for Eleanor's wedding. That would have been … would have been wonderful … Cook could cure a … cure a rash, reduce a bout of … of … ague or grippe, and … calm a cough brought on by the croup.

Oh … there were hands on her. She remembered soft hands … she had a nanny once. No, that was a dream.

For a moment she thought they were fanning her with pine boughs … were there lions at the door?

"Easy," Logan sounded close, yet far, "'twill be uncomfortable at first. But I'll be holdin' ye. Ye'll nay drown."

How many hands did he have? She felt them on her shoulders, her thighs, her feet. She dared to open one eye, only for as long as it took to reason out what was happening. Ah, there were men helping Logan carry her. Why couldn't he carry her by himself? She didn't want those other hands on her.

"No," she whispered.

Cook's voice, "Can she stand? I'll help her off with her things. Filthy rags. Hand me the clean blanket, Robert, and then ye go boil the herbs I brought. Ye best look away, Dougal."

And Logan, too, if she's going to undress me.

Why … are …

Hannah found she was unable to form words as her bare feet touched the earth. She wobbled, but Logan had his arm around her waist.

"Keep yer eyes off her, Master Logan," Cook's voice, "and take her all the way out into the deepest, coolest water."

A tug on her breeches … ugh … her shirt up over her head … was she standing at the shore, most unsteadily, in an altogether helpless state of nature?

She hadn't the strength to flail her arms or protest.

Uh ... tripping ... cold water ... a good cold on her knees ... her stomach ... her chest. Wonderful. Someone was dripping handfuls of water on her head, patting her forehead, her cheeks ... ah ...

***

LOGAN WAS MORTIFIED for her; had he been the one burning of fever and hauled into a stream naked by someone, anyone, of the opposite sex, he would have been sorely embarrassed. Lucky it was, however, that Hannah was in a state of consciousness much resembling a drunken stupor. Perhaps she wouldn't remember this indignity.

He kept his head turned enough to satisfy Cook's watchful gaze. He could only imagine if Jack were here ... the brutal comments, the teasing ... ugh, she was slipping from his grasp. He had to peek, had to move to safer footing. The rocks were coated with slime. He should have pulled his boots off; he might have gripped better with bare toes.

The water was up to his chest, swirling past yet with a gentle current. There was some risk of being swept away should he lose his footing. Hannah floated freely once he changed his grasp on her from waist to shoulders. Her feet aimed downstream, her head at his chest. He found it easiest to lightly hold her neck to keep her face above water. He patted her cheeks with handfuls of water, dripped it on her forehead, and smoothed it down her hair, the ends of which skimmed along the top of the water by her ears, like pond skeeters. He tried his best to keep his eyes trained on her nose, her closed eyelids, her hair, though his gaze gave in to temptation every time interesting parts of her rippled to the surface.

He cocked his head toward shore. Dougal stood rigidly behind Cook, not daring to face the river. Cook had lowered her large form to a rock and sat folding and unfolding the fresh blanket.

"How long will it take to break the fever?" Logan called to Cook.

She shrugged. "Could be minutes. Could be days. If she starts to shiver, bring her out."

And how was he going to do that? If she couldn't stand and walk, he'd have to carry her.

Hannah grunted. "Eleanor?"

"Nay, 'tis Logan."

"Logan?"

"Logan McKelvey. Have ye fergotten me so soon? Och, Hannah, ye're mighty ill. I beg yer pardon fer puttin' ye in such a circumstance."

"Dylan … he …"

"I ken. He's a rascal, he is." He put his lips on her forehead to test her fever then dipped her head back enough to cool the top of her head. He wanted to ask, needed to know, how she'd come to be wearing boy's clothes. She certainly hadn't left the castle wearing them. Dylan's tale did not add up.

"Nice … the water … thank you." She licked her lips. "There were lions … weren't there?"

"Ye were dreamin', lass. 'Twas a delusion. We've nay lions in Scotland, only wildcats."

Hannah's arms twitched and her entire body began to convulse.

Logan yelled to the cook, "She be shiverin'. Get the blanket ready." To Hannah he softly said, "I'm sorry, lass. We'll get ye to the castle now."

He kept one hand under her neck and felt under water for her knees. He scooped her into his arms and held her tightly against him as he picked his way carefully over the river rocks. Cook was ready with a blanket as soon as he dropped her feet to the ground. Once wrapped he picked her up again and started for the bothan.

Cook brought the raggedy clothes, grumbling about the smell of them, and Dougal followed.

"It jist began to boil," Robert said as they entered the bothan. It was tight quarters with all five of them inside.

"Out wi' ye all, 'cept Master Logan." Cook shook her head. "I shoulda brought a maid, but Dougal swore it was a lad ye were tendin'. Ye'll have to look at her in this garden o' Eden state to help me get these grimey things on her."

Logan swallowed twice rather than drool. "Aye, I've seen me sisters swimmin' afore."

***

THIS BED IS *moving*, Hannah thought. *Yet, I'm warm … comfortable … There's breathing in my ear.* She jerked awake, startling the person who held her.

"Easy," Logan's whisper sent tickles down her neck, "we're almost there. The bumpin' and jostlin' is worse in this cart, but I couldn't keep ye in the saddle wi' me."

Hannah frowned. There was an altered taste in her mouth. Not bitter or sweet. *Cinnamon?* She squirmed. "Where are we?" Behind them rode two men on horses. She craned her neck to look over Logan and see Cook driving the single horse that pulled the cart. *Poor horse.*

"Why …" she began, her frown deepening. There was a blanket thrown over her feet. She wiggled her toes underneath. Her back was against Logan's chest. *Quite nice.* His chin hovered above her left ear. *Wait, why is he shirtless?* She brought a hand up to her head. *Wet hair?* She looked down again where the blanket ended and Logan's feet stuck out. *Bare?* Needles of discomfiture stabbed at her. She felt her clothes. *Dry. Prickly.* There was a second blanket between them. A sense of dampness … "What happened?"

"Ye were feverish. Hotter than the devil's toes." The cart jerked over a dip and Logan tightened his hug. "Are ye feelin' better? Can ye remember anythin'?"

"I was sick … I …"

"Dinnae fash. Ye drank Cook's remedy. Ye should come around to yerself in a day er so."

"There are men … following us …"

"Aye, neighborin' clansmen. Friends. They believe me outta me mind and in danger o' hellfire fer tuckin' ye ag'inst me whole self and holdin' ye in me arms like this. Yer costume fooled 'em. They swear ye're a lad."

Hannah raised a hand to wave at Dougal and Robert; she didn't know them, hadn't seen them at the castle before. Her hand dropped back onto the blanket.

"I was … I … my clothes …" She blinked several times. "I was in the water … my clothes aren't wet, but yours are."

"Aye," they hit another bump and his chin brushed against her head, "I took ye in the river to break yer fever. Cook removed yer things so ye'd have somethin' dry to put on once I got ye out." He cleared his throat. "I kept me eyes averted and Dougal faced away. Robert was in the hut. Only Cook saw yer … yer loveliness."

Hannah closed her eyes. *My loveliness?* She was certain then that Logan must have peeked. There was a certain amount of heart fluttering going on in her chest as she evaluated his choice of words. The cart wobbled over some stones as they came to the gate at Castle Caladh.

Home, she thought. And then she shivered. It could never be her home. The Laird would hear of this … this indiscretion. She'd be sent away. She could only hope she'd be allowed to return to Ingledew.

Chapter 13

LAIRD MCKELVEY STOOD behind his desk in the library and stared at the missive he'd received. The original message had bounced around England and Scotland for weeks until finally being sent from Beldorney Hall to McDoon Tower to Castle Caladh. He would have liked to confer with his son Keir, but he was still traveling with his new bride.

The letter concerned the bride's friend, Hannah, who'd been recuperating in her room these last few days. He puzzled over the information. He didn't like secrets and had only learned of the plot against the King after that dreadful English redcoat had captured Keir and Eleanor. At least this secret didn't involve royalty, though it certainly involved wealth. And his own wealth and status might be affected by whatever he decided.

He lowered himself into the desk chair, an ornate, hand-carved oak piece his dear wife had commissioned for him on their first anniversary, so soon after Fenella was born. He loved his daughters and now he was forced to consider another man's daughter ... her future ... her position in life. He shook his head. He barely knew the lass. She'd been quiet in the weeks before the weddings and now she'd been shut in her room this last week. Ill, Cook said.

The Laird had noticed his younger sons' interest in the lass. Jack had perhaps lost some of that interest as he prepared for the Highland games. But Logan, he concluded, was infatuated with the girl and spent hours pacing about the castle asking Cook and the maids for news of her recovery.

There was a knock on the library door and the Laird rose, calling out permission to enter.

"Ah, dear Mary, 'tis ye who breaks me concentration."

"I'm sorry, Finley, but ye promised me another visit to the ruins. I'm sure ye said last eve that we could go this morn." Mary smiled generously at him.

"Ye've got yer heart set on makin' a home there, have ye? I'll have me men build us a proper keep and revive the Strathnaver Castle, if it pleases ye." He came around the desk and met Mary between the divan and the largest case of expensive tomes. He took both her hands in his and leaned in for a chaste kiss.

"It pleases me. Me son, Colin will thrive there and ye can hand the lairdship of Caladh over to Keir after the games, as ye planned."

"Aye." He glanced back at his desk. "Mary, what do ye ken of Hannah?"

"Oh, I was to her room a moment ago. She's recovered, but is reluctant to show herself."

"I mean what do ye ken of her past?"

Mary frowned. "Very little. She lived as a companion to me dear Eleanor since they was nay much more than bairns. A ward o' me sister, Lady Beth, is what Eleanor told me." She tilted her head and followed his gaze to the letter on his desk. "Why do ye ask?"

He hesitated a moment. "Och, I've learnt of her family."

"Her family?"

"Aye. Stolen, she was. Her father, of the landed gentry, a tradesman of some means, has been lookin' fer her nigh unto twelve years."

Mary put a hand over her mouth, eyes wide. "Stolen?" She shook her head. "Lord Edgeworth nay doubt had a hand in it."

"Can ye bring her down to me? I needs speak wi' the lass."

"Certainly. I'll help her dress and bring her to ye."

No sooner had Mary gone out of the library than Logan burst in.

"Father. Dylan McDoon has dared to show his face here. He returned me horse and now stands in the bailey, claimin' he's come fer Hannah." Logan's face was fiery red beneath several days' growth of beard.

"Fer Hannah? What has he to do wi' the lass?" The Laird moved back toward his desk.

"Ye ken she was lost on his watch. They went ridin' together. He left her beside the road. An' ye sent a dozen men out to help find her. Father, it's nay like ye to ferget."

The Laird slowly lowered himself into his chair. "I've had much on me mind. I've been negotiatin' with ole McDoon to get Jack betrothed to wee Megan McDoon." His face twitched. "Are ye meanin' he … deflowered her? And now means to take her to wife?"

Logan paced toward the desk, then turned and walked to a bookcase. He ran a finger down the spine of a leather-bound Bible, pivoted, and faced the desk again. "I pray that dinnae happen … but … I ken she's of the servant class … I ken ye expect me to accept a betrothal of yer choosin', but I … I choose Hannah."

Laird McKelvey picked up the letter. "Son, ye understand ye're meant to wed a Scottish lass. I relented with Keir, but I cannae let ye make the same mistake. Besides …" he waved the letter, "she's English gentry. I'm obliged to return her to England."

"Gentry?" Logan's brows pulled together. "Nay. She was Eleanor's companion. A maid. A servant. The farthest thing from British aristocracy."

"See here." The Laird set the letter down, smoothed it out, and pointed at the elegant strokes of ink.

***

"THE LAIRD HIMSELF desires to speak with me?" Hannah rose from the divan and faced Mary. "But why?"

"I'm sure he'll tell ye. I'll help ye out o' that dressin' robe and into a day dress." Mary went to the wardrobe and opened it.

There was a knock and Elspeth let herself in. "Pardon me, Mistress, but there be a young lord at the door, askin' fer ye." She smiled at Hannah and then spotted Mary. "Oh, Mrs. Mcfarlane, I dinnae see ye there." She curtsied. "Please, let me help her into somethin' else … somethin' more fittin' fer a proposal." She giggled.

Mary put a hand out. "Wait. What do ye mean? Proposal?"

"Aye. The young McDoon is here to take Mistress Hannah to McDoon Tower. He says his father insists." She bit her lip and whispered, "He seemed verra nervous. He went back to pacin' his horses around the bailey." She glanced at the ladies. "Oh, Mistress Hannah, ye look as pale as the young lord."

Mary clapped her hands to get Elspeth to look at her. "Thank ye, Elspeth. I'll help Hannah."

Alone again, Mary held the dress out. "So ... ye've got a suitor and methinks ye're of a mind to be ill again."

"Dylan McDoon ... he can't want to marry a servant, can he?"

"Did he have his way wi' ye?"

"No!"

"Then save yer worries fer another day. The good Laird of Castle Caladh willnae let ye leave wi' the scoundrel. I 'ave a wee bit o' influence." She nodded at what Hannah was wearing and Hannah started pulling it off. "Hannah, do ye remember how ye came aboot to be at Ingledew? Ye ken, doan ye, that Lady Beth is me half-sister?"

"Mm-hm." Hannah set the dressing gown over a chair back and stepped into the day dress. Mary pulled it up and started lacing the back. "I was brought from Cornwall to be Eleanor's companion."

"Who brought ye?"

Hannah stared upward. "Mm. Two men and a woman that smelled of lavender. I remember I cried the whole journey. Then we arrived at the biggest home I'd ever seen. I met the Lord and Lady and then Eleanor. I told her I was Hannah Pascoe of Feock, Cornwall. Lady Beth slapped me and told me to never mention Cornwall again." She gave a single huff of a laugh. "But Eleanor told me to never forget it."

"How old were ye?"

"I don't know. Six or seven, I suppose."

"There. Ye're all laced and buttoned. I'll take ye to the Laird."

"But what about Dylan McDoon?"

"Let 'im stew in the bailey. The Laird has important things to tell ye first."

***

MARY AND HANNAH stood outside the library door listening to the loud voices within.

Mary crinkled her nose. "Perhaps ye should wait in the other room. 'Tis a more pleasant space. The McKelvey crest is worth a gaze."

Hannah nodded and followed Mary into the elaborate room; her eyes immediately went to the corner where the secret panel was. She took a seat on a divan across from Mary.

Mary chattered on about Eleanor and Colin and the Laird and his sons, but even though Hannah responded as politely as she could, her thoughts returned to the hidden staircase, the tower, and the kisses she enjoyed there with Logan.

And then her spirits plummeted. There was no hope of being with Logan. She feared her fate was with Dylan McDoon, to be bound to him and subject to his abuse. But ... but ... it didn't make much sense that he would want to marry her. Had she misjudged his actions? Was tying her to the horse and speaking with such menace only an impulsive jest? If she hadn't hidden up the tree, might he have laughed and explained 'twas all a joke? She'd been confused and surprised before by other men's senseless words or actions. And her first impressions of some men changed completely after a bit ... coming to mind were Captain Luxbury, Tavish, and even Keir and Logan. The captain she thought was good turned out to be bad and the others she thought bad were good.

"I'll see if they've finished their discussion." Mary stood and walked across the rug.

Hannah sighed as she heard the voices grow louder as soon as Mary opened one door and then the other. She could clearly hear the argument continuing. She moved closer to the door to listen. Mary's voice broke in. She explained where Hannah was waiting. The argument resumed between father and son and Logan's tone changed to supplication. He asked his father for a moment alone first and when she heard the Laird agree, she rushed to sit down again. Seconds later he appeared at the door, closed it, and hurried to her.

"Hannah. Are ye recovered, lass? I feared fer yer life." He dropped himself onto the cushion and pulled her into an embrace.

She winced. "And I fear for it now that you're about to crush that life from my ribs." She lifted her face to his.

He loosened the hug only enough to allow them space to stare into each other's eyes.

"I love ye, lass. I fought wi' me father fer the right to wed ye. Ye must ken that it matters nary a whit to me whether ye're a milk maid or a princess."

Hannah spoke without thinking. "And I love you, Logan McKelvey. I loved you when I didn't know you were a laird's son. I thought you were an insurrectionist from the class of ... of the laboring poor. Someone of my class, perhaps." She laughed. "Until I heard you and Keir talking of his betrothal and dowries. And then I knew there was no hope."

"Don't say that."

"But it's true. Your father will never betroth you to a commoner."

"Ye're nay commoner, Hannah. And that rascal McDoon is here to claim ye. Would ye rather be bound to me or to him?"

Hannah whispered, "You," her heart pumping harder now.

Logan raised his eyes to the tapestry. The family crest had symbols including strength, valor, and courage. Two braided cords hung down on either side, long red plaits knotted at the ends.

"I have an idea. Do ye trust me?"

"I do."

Logan released her and stepped to the large rug that covered a trap door. He lifted one edge and gave it a shake. It settled down out of place and he pushed it back with his toe to crumple it more. He took the dirk from his waist and, to Hannah's surprise, sliced the red cords off the tapestry. She furrowed her brow, but when he gestured to her to join him at the secret panel she quickly moved to his side.

"But won't your father know where we've gone?" Hannah trembled as she went through the opening with him. The winding stone steps before her didn't look as steep today. The scent of wood and mildew this time was familiar and pleasant.

"I wrinkled the rug; he'll think I took ye down to the cellar and out through the passageway there. He'll send men to catch us where it comes out, but we'll be here all along."

She eyed the lengths of red cords in his hand. She hadn't questioned his action when he cut them free of the crest.

"Come. Let's climb up and I'll tell ye me plan."

They reached the top. Light streamed across the walls and in this present moment the circular space felt pacifying, safe. Logan took her hand and pulled her to the far side where there were no lookout holes and only a short bench to rest on. She sat and he pressed in close to her.

"I must tell ye … me father has a letter … from yer father. He's been asearchin' fer ye all yer life, Hannah. Ye're Hannah Pascoe of Feock, Cornwall."

"Yes, I know who I am."

"But do ye ken the Pascoes of Cornwall are an important family? Rich. Of high status. Ye were sold to Lord Edgeworth of Ingledew. He was hidin' Eleanor, a royal descendent—"

"I know of Eleanor's true parentage."

"But ye dinnae ken o' yers. Lord Edgeworth couldnae give Eleanor a companion of low birth. He bought ye because ye were of the upper class."

Hannah stared. It was too much to believe. She huffed, tried to smile, frowned more deeply, and then realized she was squeezing Logan's hands with all her strength and gulping down streams of saliva.

"Ye see, Dylan came not only to return me horse, but to claim ye. The letter what tells of this strange truth arrived with him."

Hannah lightened her grip on him and lowered her eyes to her lap. She swallowed hard; she needed to ponder a bit these revelations. After a few moments she let go of Logan's hands and stood up.

"He's out there, isn't he? Waiting." She crossed the space and found a lookout peephole angled downward. Someone, long ago, had chiseled through the thickness to provide her with exactly the view she wanted. The courtyard within the bailey held movement. The young McDoon paced around, leading two saddled horses and one—she recognized it as the mount she'd ridden on—unsaddled.

"He's there. He's trading back the horse you won from him … Toaty. That's its name. He's trading Toaty for me."

Logan eliminated the space between them. "He coulda brought a thousand stallions and I wouldnae let ye go." He took her in his arms. "Hannah, I love ye and if ye'll have me, we can be married right now, right here."

She let herself sink into his embrace. "How can that be?"

He glanced back at the cords he left on the bench. "Handfasting."

"I don't understand."

"Come." He pulled her back to the bench, retrieved the cords, and said, "'Tis bindin', as bindin' as a weddin' ceremony. Me sister, Elsie, did handfast herself to Charles after the sad passin' of our vicar. They lived together as husband and wife until a new vicar came, the ceremony bein' as official as a weddin' ... so they had nae worry o' havin' a bastard bairn 'cause o' the handfastin'."

She'd heard the term, but never gave it much thought. Her fingers were ice cold, her chest constricted around a heart beating too fast. Could this be the answer? What would the consequence be? There must be some kind of punishment to be endured if they had to do this handfasting ceremony in secret.

"I ..." she had no words.

Logan lifted her left hand. The warmth of his was undeniably comforting.

"Will ye have me, Hannah?"

She gulped. Nodded. Offered her face upward. He kissed her with such gentleness that she thought she must be floating. "I'll have you, Logan McKelvey, if it means I'll be your wife for all of time."

"Aye. For all of time."

Their hands were still clasped between them, left to left. He lifted the cords. "Take one. 'Twould be easier if someone were here to make the knots, but we can do it together." He wound his cord around their joined hands twice and tucked one end under the other then pulled it tight with his teeth and right hand. He repeated that to form a knot.

"Hannah, I take ye fer me wife. I love ye, lass. I will care fer ye all me days. Protect ye. Care fer ye. Love ye always." He tapped the knot and looked into her eyes. He placed his right palm on their fastened hands.

Hannah smiled up at him and he lifted his free hand to place it against her cheek. She closed her eyes and nuzzled her face into his warm palm.

"'Tis yer turn, me love."

She put her cord around their hands as he had, made a tight knot, and said, "Logan, I'll be your wife for all my days. I'll obey you and have your children and stand at your side no matter the trouble. I love you. I love you." She leaned in, their hands tightly between them, a knotted lump of fists and fingers pressing against their flesh. She felt the galloping of his heart through her hand, knew he was sensing her breathless throbbing, knew also that he was going to kiss her now and that it might possibly last forever. His free hand went around her shoulders and she did the same. Their lips met. Trembling at first. Light and expectant and soft. And then … more insistent. Deeper. A thorough kiss.

Chapter 14

LOGAN FACED HANNAH and took the steps down backwards since their hands were still tied together. He needed to show his father what they'd done. He smiled up at her, taking each step slowly, his right hand on the rough inner wall and her right hand giving her support on the outer wall of the confined space.

The voice they heard when they almost reached the bottom was Jack's.

"Aha! 'Tis as I thought. Ye hid her— Ho! Are ye tied together?" Jack grabbed at Logan's shoulder as he reached the bottom. It was cramped and darker in the space between stair and panel with a stronger, more pungent smell of wetness. "What have ye done, Logan?"

Logan lifted their hands, the cords and knots dangling. "We're handfasted."

Jack stared open-mouthed from his brother's smirking face to Hannah's shy smile. As they lowered their arms Jack asked, "Ye did so, Hannah, of yer own free will?"

She gave the slightest of nods and he stepped back abruptly and pulled the panel open. "I'll stand wi' ye, Logan, as ye face our father."

Logan thanked him and ushered Hannah through. He wrapped his free arm around her and they walked in tandem through the room, Jack trailing.

Logan took a deep breath before entering the library.

"Father—"

"Ah, ye've brought the lass." The Laird stood at his desk and picked up a thick piece of rag paper. "I've written me answer. Did ye tell her?" He raised his eyes and his gaze roamed from their faces to their knotted wrists. Jack stood by the door, arms folded and a curious look on his face. Understanding dawned on the old laird and his expression changed.

"Aye, Father, I told her … and we … we pledged ourselves to each other. I intend to take her to England … to meet her family, at last." His lips twitched.

The Laird slammed his fists against the desktop. "Do ye now? Ye're still a pup, lad." He ripped up the paper. "So ye intend, ye say, to take her to Cornwall, eh?" He set his jaw and stared.

"Aye."

"And ye've thought this through, have ye?"

Logan hesitated only a tick. "Aye, 'tis all I've had on me mind. First, I'll speak wi' McDoon, take me wagered horse back and send him on his way."

Jack interrupted. "And blacken his eyes. I'll help ye."

"Aye," Logan snickered, "and then we'll pack a trunk, some weapons and food," his voice grew louder, "and borrow yer second coach and I believe both Robert and Dougal would accept a modest wage to accompany us … for safety."

The Laird stared, still snorting deep breaths through his nose, his lips tightly sealed as he listened.

"Sir?" Hannah's single syllable was honey soft.

The Laird shifted his attention to her.

"May I see the letter?"

Laird McKelvey said nothing. He motioned her forward and pushed the letter across the desk. Hannah and Logan walked in step. She reached for the letter and held it up to read. As tears began to stream down her cheeks, Logan held her all the more tightly.

***

JACK LEFT THE room when his brother and his new wife examined the letter. He wasn't upset or disappointed. He liked Hannah, but he knew from the beginning that he'd lose out to Logan. He walked out into the courtyard and marched up to Dylan.

"I'll take me brother's horse to the stable."

When Dylan held out the reins with one hand, the other hand occupied with the reins of the two saddled horses, Jack took advantage and swung a hard fist at Dylan's jaw. Dylan stumbled back into the chest of one of the horses, dropping all the leather straps and ending up on his back.

Jack grabbed the mare, spit on the ground, and used a Gaelic curse and threat to warn Dylan to leave. "And doan think ye'll be welcome at the games this summer. Or that I'd ever consider marryin' yer sister, Megan."

Dylan peered up, elbows braced on the ground, his horses well back and nibbling freely on whatever weeds they could find. "Och, ye'll change yer mind." He rolled onto his knees and stood up. "I challenge ye now, Jack McKelvey, for a fair fight at the games. Ye best learn how to handle a *claidheamh mòr*."

"Git yerself gone, McDoon, or Logan'll be out here next to teach ye what happens when ye take a lady ridin' and leave her aside the road."

"I'm nay leavin' 'til I see Hannah. I mean to make me apologies and ask fer her hand."

Jack shook his head. "Ha! Ye're too late. Her hand is bound tight to Logan's. The deed's done."

Dylan frowned, wiped his hands on his kilt. "What deed?"

"They've been handfasted. Wed, they be. A year and a day and 'twill be solemnly bound."

Dylan stared open-mouthed at Jack, then a smirk spread from lip to eye, and he grunted. "'Twon't last. She's naught but a common English maid."

"An English lady, ye mean. I ken o' the letter."

Dylan laughed wryly. "I learnt enough o' the lass to pen that letter meself." He pulled one of the horses to him. "It fooled me own father and I suspect it fooled yers. I meant to steal 'er from yer brother." He mounted the horse and pulled him back until he could catch the bridle of the other one.

121

"Ye're lyin'," Jack said, then lower, under his breath as Dylan trotted away, "I ken ye're lyin', ye mingin bawbag."

Jack chased after the mare who lifted her head from the grasses and started to follow the other horses. He caught a loose rein and led her to the stable. He didn't know what to do about that bit of information. If Dylan wasn't lying and the letter truly was a ruse, invented by that mischief-maker, then he should tell Logan of this falsity and save them a useless trip to England.

But he had to be lying. He must be. It was how he meant to punch back, to cast doubt. He stabled the horse and hurried back to the castle, intending to get hold of that letter and examine it well.

***

"'TIS ENOUGH," HANNAH said, her head pressed against Logan's shoulder, "'tis enough to know. You needn't go to the expense of a journey."

Mary, who'd been sitting in a corner of the great library, trying to be inconspicuous, left her seat to join them across from the Laird.

"Finley, I'd like to go wi' them, if ye'd be so kind as to keep Colin here. I remember England well enough to be of help to them."

The Laird softened his expression as he answered her. "Mary, I dinnae want to let ye outta me sight. Ye've become too precious to me." He glanced at Hannah. "But ... the lass should have a chaperone. I'd go meself, but I have much to do in preparation for the Highland games, but six weeks away."

"Thank ye, father," Logan quickly said, "but as she's me wife now there be nay need for a chaperone."

"I wouldn't mind, but please, it's too much fuss." Hannah tried to smile, but it didn't take; her mouth soon turned down at the edges. She yanked on the cords that bound her to Logan. A wave of heat came over her and she shuddered involuntarily.

"'Tis nay fuss, me love." He pulled his dirk out and carefully put the tip between his own flesh and the cords. A single swipe and they were free. The cords dropped to the stone floor and he retrieved them, placed them in Hannah's hand, and said, "These be a symbol fer now, but I'll cover ye with rings and jewels soon enough."

Hannah squeezed her fingers over the cords and wondered what Eleanor would think of this hasty handfasting.

Jack burst through the doorway. "I sent yon scoundrel away, but nay afore I had a square go at him and broke his face." All eyes went to him. "I needs see that letter he brought."

"Ye clyped 'im?" Logan gave him a congratulatory shove as he reached the desk.

"Aye, and I took back yer mare fer ye. Now, the letter?" He pushed the ripped papers aside and picked up the letter, ignoring the subtle growl his father made. He folded the letter up without looking at the contents. He was more interested in the four wax seals, each embossed and broken.

"What's the matter with the letter?" Logan frowned at him. "We've been studyin' it. But Hannah dinnae ken her father's first name."

Hannah swiped a finger under one eye to blot the wetness there.

"The McDoon claimed to have written it himself. To fool his father into thinkin' the lass has a fortune and worth it to marry her … and then to fool our father into lettin' him take her away. But," he pointed to the seals, "the first two seals are unfamiliar to me, then there's the Beldorney crest. Ye ken it, aye father? Followed by the McDoon tower crest. The edges are all worn as they would be, bein' carried in different satchels from England to Scotland, and from Hall to Tower to Castle."

Laird McKelvey took the letter and did his own examination and handed it to Logan who checked the first broken waxed seal against the inked seal beneath the letter's signature: Nathaniel Pascoe. "Look, Hannah. Dinnae fash. Dylan is disreputable and untrustworthy. 'Tis only another of his tall tales and blatant untruths. I believe the letter's real. Try to remember yer father's name. Was it Nathaniel?"

"I don't know." She wrung her hands, twisting the cords, and looked to Mary for help.

"Leave the lass alone. Ye're all upsettin' her. Come along, Hannah, we'll help each other pack." Mary put an arm around her and hustled her out to the stairs.

"Ye seemed a might overwhelmed. I saw the same expression on me dear Eleanor's face the night before she wed Finley's son." They started up the stairs.

Hannah sniffled. "It seemed the right thing to do … the handfasting. I do love Logan."

"I believe ye. I ken how fast a woman can succumb to a McKelvey's attention." She punctuated the thought with a light laugh. "I thought we might have a few words alone … as ye have no mother to … uh … to tell ye what to expect on yer weddin' night, mm … I'll tell ye what I told Eleanor."

***

"I WON'T SAY I have doubts about any of the McKelvey men, but I see how powerful the clan is. I think it best ye do as Eleanor did and have yer union blessed by a priest or a vicar." Mary patted down the last of the things they'd put in the trunk they would share for the journey. Every stitch of clothing had come from the generosity of the McKelvey sisters, all married off and out of the castle now. "Me own story may have a happy ending at last, but ye ken I was married to the third son of King George the Second and Caroline … and we had to keep it secret. But all those empty years after his death … well, I had the proof, the parchments that told the truth … until me daughter burned them."

Hannah closed the trunk. "And then Keir went in search of the originals and found them."

"Aye. A good lad he is. Eleanor chose wisely."

"But she *is* of royal blood, and I am not. A handfasting will do for me."

The long-lost English accent came back to Mary's lips. "No, Hannah, you mustn't rely on a promise that had no witnesses. You must convince young Logan to stop when we pass a kirk or in England a church … I know just the one … and then you'll have me as your witness. With so many McKelvey heirs, your children—"

Hannah stopped her with a hand on her wrist. "I will think on what you say, though I think I can trust Logan."

"Yes … aye, of course … but doan … do not … go to his room tonight. Wait to consummate your marriage until you have that parchment."

Hannah frowned, but Mary's words had a calming effect. The tears and shivers and prickly heat she'd felt in the library were absent now and relief and comfort spread through her being. A parchment, a contract of marriage, something more binding perhaps than tasseled cords.

A timid knock came at the door and Elspeth peeked in. "Do ye need me help? The Laird asked me to see to yer wants." She came all the way in holding a curious-looking box. "I brought this to hold your necessaries. The Laird's dear departed wife had it especially built. 'Tis contrived to hold yer tweezers, nail nippers, brushes and combs, sewing needles an' even powder an' oil." She opened the box and Hannah and Mary scrutinized the wooden indentations meant to compartmentalize each item.

"Mm," Hannah sniffed, "what's that smell?"

"'Tis cedar wood," Mary answered and Elspeth nodded.

"I wish ye much happiness." Elspeth handed the box to Hannah. She withdrew from her apron a finely embroidered kerchief. "Please accept this as me gift to ye and Master Logan. A thousand blessin's to ye, may ye be healthy all your days. May ye have long life and peace, may ye both grow old with goodness, and with riches." She curtsied as Hannah accepted the gift.

"Thank you, Elspeth."

"'Twas me pleasure." She curtsied again and said, "The Laird told Cook to make a feast fer ye tonight. Is there anythin' special you'd be wantin'?"

"Oh," Hannah was stunned, "I ... I like all of Cook's meals ... but if there's rabbit, I know that Logan prefers it."

***

LOGAN ESCORTED HANNAH to dinner. There were only six place settings, all at one end of the long table. Logan nodded at his father, then at Jack, Mary, and Colin. It was an intimate marriage feast, nothing like what was presented at Keir and Eleanor's banquet, but all his favorites were set out: jugged hare, links of sausage, spring onions and greens, sweetened rhubarb, and pease pudding.

"Were ye expectin' bubbly-jock?"

"Aye, brother, I was." He held the chair for Hannah as she sat.

"'Tis what I'll have at me weddin' feast ... someday. But I believe all the turkeys in the pen were roasted for our brother's spread. A shame he was too busy wi' that hen o' his to enjoy that dinner." Jack smirked. A look passed between the brothers and Logan sat down.

Jack continued speaking as two servants stepped up to fill the bride and groom's plates. "I ken ye wanted Dougal and Robert to accompany ye, but Robert's our best man for the log toss and should stay behind to practice. I'll take his place as me specialty in the Highland games is the axe throw. I can practice wherever we camp or lodge."

"Camp?" Mary gasped.

125

"Nay," the Laird's voice boomed. He brought it down a notch to add, "I'll give ye coin enough to stay at inns along the way. I'll nay have Mary—or Hannah—sleepin' in a bothan or out in the woods."

"I have sufficient coin, Father. And Jack, I'll take ye up on yer offer. I'd be pleased to have ye along."

Logan smiled at Hannah. "What do ye think of the rabbit? Be it to yer likin'?"

She gulped and nodded. "I've never tasted better."

There was agreement around the table and then the Laird made a toast to the couple. The rest of the meal was eaten with great relish and much laughter as Jack told stories about Logan and the Laird interspersed them with his own recollections of his son's successes and prowess in last year's Highland games.

Once all appetites were sated, Colin, who'd been as quiet as Hannah throughout, begged to spend the rest of the evening with the stable lad. Laird McKelvey took Mary to the library and only Jack remained at the table with his brother and Hannah.

"Ye should also ken, Hannah, that Logan snores. Ye'll be up all night, I fear." He winked at his brother and added, "But ye can rest in the carriage tomorrow. I'll have Elspeth fill it wi' pillows."

Logan fiddled with his spoon and tried to give 'go away' hints to Jack. He had something he wanted to say privately to Hannah, but his brother didn't seem to want to leave the table.

Hannah made a show of sipping the last drops of her wine.

Logan called out, "Elspeth! Bring another bottle."

"Oh … no. No, if I have any more, I'll fall asleep before the sun sets."

Jack guffawed. "Ye doan want that, brother."

Logan glared at Jack. "The bottle's fer *ye*, Jack." He rose and held a hand out for Hannah. "Let's take a stroll, shall we, Hannah?"

She rested her hand on his arm. They exchanged smiles and he felt his heart swell. He had no doubt at all that he'd done the right thing in suggesting they be handfasted. She was his now, but more than that, he realized, he belonged to her. He hadn't expected to feel this remarkable connection. The idea of handfasting had always been, in his mind, a subordinate event to an actual wedding, but he no longer believed that. This woman was his wife, his mate, his partner. He looked down at the smooth skin of her hand, imagined the marks of the cords though they

126

had faded, and thought of the words, the vows, they'd said to one another. And then he noticed something in her aspect. The lass was hesitant, but eager. Afraid, but brave. Excited, but timid.

He led her out to the garden.

"Did ye enjoy our dinner?" He put one hand on hers.

"Of course."

"And are ye ready fer our journey on the morrow?" He took her to one of the benches that had been recently built. They sat, hands still touching. The evening air sneaked around them with hints of night-blooming jasmine on its breath.

"Yes. Mary and I filled a trunk and Elspeth brought us a box for personal things. It was your mother's. I hope you don't mind."

He shook his head, intent more on what would come next. Should he kiss her? Or should he speak of love? Or—and this was what his heart was prompting him to do—should he tell her what he suspected?

"Hannah?"

"Yes, Logan." She spoke his name with a sigh.

"I'm verra glad we did what we did and said what we said ... but ... I'm yer husband now, ye ken, and ... as yer husband I expect certain things to happen between us." He looked at her and she raised her eyes to his. He saw in her gaze what he'd predicted from her silence at dinner: she was unsettled and uncertain. "I think it best if we wait ... if we wait until ... well, I ken the handfastin' be legal and all, but I swear, on me dead mother's grave, that I'll nay touch ye as yer husband until we're blessed in a kirk, if that be what ye want."

Her response was not what he expected. She threw her arms around him and gave him a deeper kiss than he thought possible. She dropped her embrace, their lips parted, and she leaned back enough to speak softly. Her breathing was heavy though and the words came out in a rush, "I'm yer wife, Logan McKelvey, and wife I'll be ... tonight and forever."

Chapter 15

H OW THOUGHTFUL," MARY said as she climbed into the
carriage after Hannah. "I dinnae … did not … expect to be
cushioned on this journey." She plumped a pillow and sat upon
it.

Hannah smiled shyly at Mary, wanting to say something, but keeping
her secret private instead. Last night Logan had been … ah, she could
never describe it, not even to Eleanor, though Eleanor would have
discerned the truth from Hannah's happy mood. It was strange, though,
that she didn't miss Eleanor as much today.

Jack poked his head in the door. "Logan's climbin' up into the
driver's seat now. I'll be ridin' behind and Dougal's out front. Ye've nay
need to be scared as we have pistols and swords." He patted his kilt,
making the dirk and the axe attached to his belt wiggle. "And these tartan
colors will ward off highwaymen and beggars."

The ladies nodded, but Mary said, "I hope ye've brought breeches
along for when we pass into England. We'll get a better reception if we
look English."

"Aye, we've thought o' that."

Jack closed the door and yelled something to Logan, then mounted his horse. Hannah could hear him behind the carriage. This was not the carriage she was in when she first came to Castle Caladh. This carriage smelled of flowers and cedar. There was ornate paneling inside and red corded curtains over windows that held no glass. She wondered how often this carriage was used; it appeared fancy but not new.

"If I remember me … my … journey from England so long ago, we'll be bobbin' around in here for three days at least." Mary folded her hands in her lap then immediately pressed one against the side as the carriage lurched forward. Hannah, too, caught her balance by grabbing onto the window sill.

It wasn't long before Hannah noticed how pale Mary had become and called out the window for Logan to stop. Mary stepped out and walked about until the motion sickness subsided. The journey continued in short spurts as the ride grew more jarring and unpleasant. They stopped often to allow Mary to recover her equilibrium. On the better roadways they managed to travel for longer lengths of time. Hannah commented on the landscapes they passed, the early summer fields, the swan-filled lochs, the moors and glens. Mary looked out when she could do so without feeling nauseated. They were still in Scotland when they stopped at an inn the first night.

Logan had Dougal and Jack see to the horses as he procured three rooms. The inn provided a modest supper and then Logan took some candles from the table and escorted Mary to her room and Hannah to theirs. Hannah's insides tickled with the thought of another night alone with Logan.

"I'll be a wee bit late," he said, handing Hannah a candle. "'Tis Dougal's job to see there be no thievery of our carriage, our horses, or yer trunk. But I'll stay too so he can sleep a while, then Jack'll relieve me after midnight."

"It sounds like you and Jack are the guards and not Dougal." She touched his arm with casual intimacy.

"Aye, but 'tis best to have two swords and two pistols at the ready, even if ye have to wake the eyes and arms of one." He put a finger under her chin and tipped her head up for a kiss. "Lock the door." He gave her another kiss. "If ye'd feel safer in Mary's room …"

"No, I'll be fine." The candle light danced across her face. He kissed her again and she couldn't wait for midnight.

He reached for the dirk in his belt. "Here. Take this, but when ye hear me voice at the door, don't be ready to tickle me ribs with it." He laid the handle of the dirk in her other hand, the blade shimmering in the low light.

He pushed the door open for her and she entered, set the candle on a night stand, and turned toward him. She didn't want him to go. She glanced at the quilted bed; it was half the size of the beds at Caladh. The thought of sleeping—or not sleeping—on the modest straw mattress sent another thrill through her chest.

Logan was grinning at her, but he pulled the door closed with a final word to lock it. Once closed, she heard his voice whisper goodnight.

Hannah stood still a moment more before twisting the iron key in the lock and setting it on the table next to the candle. She looked about the small room, clutching the knife. There was a window and it was open to the warm evening. Since this room was on the second floor, there was no need for her to feel unsafe, but nevertheless, she closed it. The corner held a three-legged chair, four hooks on the wall, and another nightstand with a bowl of water and a ratty towel. A chamber pot sat next to the fireplace. There'd be no need for a fire tonight or any night this summer.

She undressed down to her chemise and crawled under the covers. They stank of sweat and cheap perfume, but she barely noticed. Her thoughts were on Logan.

***

LOGAN LAUGHED WHEN he saw what Dougal and Jack were doing. They'd set a lantern next to a tree and were taking turns throwing their axes at the tree trunk. Jack's two-handed form succeeded in striking and sticking in the bark each time, while Dougal's efforts were failures four times out of five.

"Och, ye're a puny devil wi' the axe, Dougal. Me brother'll take the prize this year, fer sure."

The men laughed, retrieved their axes, and walked back to Logan.

"Let's see how ye fare, Logan." Jack raised his brow and eyed the axe at Logan's waist. Dougal popped his axe into a loop on his belt.

Logan took his stance. "The trick, Dougal, is not to flick yer wrist or over-spin." His arms held the axe steady over his head, elbows bent. His focus didn't waver from the target, not even when the crunching sound of heavy boots breaking sticks reached his ears. The axe flew forward, head over handle three times, and struck the trunk dead center and held. "Like that." He turned and the grin left his face in the instant it took to see a tall lad approaching.

"Dinnae fash, Logan. I hired him to take the first watch. We three shall wet our tongues in yon pub."

Logan, Jack, and Dougal stepped into the pub, the only one in the small village, hardly expecting to find danger within the cramped and smokey walls. The heavy, wooden door clanged behind them as they stepped into the shadows.

The air was gray and thick with the smell of sweat, ale, and pipe smoke. The noise of laughter, clanking mugs, and raucous conversation swelled in the dimly lit room. Logan could just make out the forms of the men, half of them crowded around tables and the other half, drunk or sleeping, scattered across the floor.

In the furthest corner of the pub, he spotted a free table. But as they moved toward it, the conversation died away, and a heavy silence fell across the room. Their presence drew a substantial chill.

Four large Scotsmen rose from the shadows, their eyes narrowed and they touched the axes tucked haphazardly into their belts. Jack and Dougal stopped in their tracks as the leader of the quartet pointed to them. Logan kept walking.

"Ye'd best be heading out of here," he growled. "This is no place for yer kind."

Logan stopped then and glanced back at Dougal, who met his gaze with a resigned expression, but Jack stepped forward and with his brother faced the angry Scotsman, who had folded his thick arms across his chest.

"I said, ye'd best be headin' out," he growled again.

Logan felt a wave of anger rising within him, but he bit his tongue and remained where he was.

"I think the good fellow be right," Dougal said quietly.

Jack clenched his fists, stifling his rage, as the Scotsman stepped closer. Logan reached into his sporan and pulled out a handful of coins, tossing them on the table, and stating loudly, "An ale for any man who'll drink with a McKelvey."

131

"Nay," the big man said. "I told ye ... take yer leave. This pub be fer McIntyres, McMillans, an' Browns. Ye've nay been invited. Now ye'll pay for yer arrogance."

Logan hesitated for a moment, before tonight he would have faced a challenge, but with Hannah to think of, and Mary, too, he chose a different response. Jack and Dougal turned and started toward the door. Logan reached to scooped up his coins. But as he did, the Scotsman reached for his axe.

"Leave them," he snarled.

Jack and Dougal stopped. The Scotsman stepped forward, a menacing glint in his eye, his right hand on the axe handle. Logan met him eye to eye then edged backwards, his hand instinctively reaching for his own axe. But as he did, the Scotsman laughed and raised his weapon.

"Ye can't out-axe me, lad," he said. "Now ye'll learn what it means to anger a McMillan."

Jack and Dougal exchanged a look. They knew that this was a fight neither of them could win, but if Logan was as good as he was but minutes ago ...

The angry Scotsman raised his axe. Logan pulled out his.

"Come on then. Let's see what ye've got." The Scotsman grinned and brought his axe down, slicing through the air with a menacing whoosh. Jack and Dougal both leaped back, barely avoiding the blade. The Scotsman and his cohorts moved closer, their axes held ready.

"'Tis a contest ye want, 'twill be a contest ye get." Logan stated.

A few of the drunken men on the ground crawled to the darker corners of the room. Two men picked up a table and tilted it on its side. They dragged an unconscious drunk to it and draped him over the edge, his head and arms hanging over and leaving only a few spots for an axe to strike. He looked like a piece of laundry hung on a line to dry.

"All right, then, McKelvey, let us see if ye be brave enough and true enough to land yer axe on wood."

"Aye!" another man shouted. "'Tis a feat we've seen our own McMillan do."

Logan shook his head. "I'll nay aim at a man. Draw his outline with a piece o' charcoal."

132

The pub men all laughed. McMillan snorted. "Aye, if ye're unsure of yer skill." He motioned to one of his men. "Push him off. Make a circle where his head be hangin'."

Logan let his breath out and clutched his axe more tightly. He signaled to Jack and Dougal. They split off to opposite sides of the room, their eyes darting around on the lookout for threatening moves.

McMillan nodded once the drunk was pulled off and the circle drawn. "Ye get three tries to put yer axe in the center."

Logan wiped the blade against his kilt, breathed out, and lifted the axe over his head. Before he threw it, the Scotsman came at him, blade high and ready to swing. Suddenly blades were swishing the air on all sides and his brother and Dougal entered the fray. Weaving and ducking was the best way to avoid the dangerous swipes. Most of the pub's customers fled the room, pulling drunken or sleeping friends with them. The men's axes clanged or thumped when metal met blade or wood. The fight was four against three, with Logan swinging and spinning and swerving to hold off two at once until Jack kicked the legs out from under one of them. Then he faced McMillan, swore a Gaelic curse, and jumped to the side as the big man swung. The man stumbled and fell, dropping his axe in the process. Logan bent down and picked it up, pointing it directly at the Scotsman's face.

"Run," he said, his voice cold and menacing.

The other three Scotsmen suddenly lost their nerve and left. Without his three comrades, McMillan scrambled to his feet and bolted out of the pub, leaving Dougal and the McKelvey brothers alone.

Logan dropped the man's axe, his hands trembling from the adrenaline. He turned to Dougal, who was nursing a bloody gash on his arm.

"Are ye goin' to die on us?" he asked.

Dougal shook his head, his expression grim.

"I'll live," he said. "But I think we'd best be on our way. We've stirred up trouble here."

Logan nodded. He helped Dougal to his feet, and together with Jack, they made their way out of the pub.

***

HANNAH'S HEART WAS pounding as she heard the desperate cries for help coming from the small room next to hers. She knew it was

Mary's voice, and that Mary was in danger. Hannah threw off the blanket, grabbed the dirk, and unlocked her own door. She rushed into the hall and saw how the lock on Mary's door was broken. Her hand shook as she tried to grab the handle. When her fingers found it, she pushed the door open.

Inside the room a man, tall and menacing, stood with his arms wrapped tightly around Mary. A single candle made it hard to see Mary's face, but she could tell it was twisted in fear and pain and the top of her chemise was ripped.

There was no time to think. Hannah charged forward and plunged the knife into the man's arm. He screamed in pain, but did not release his grip on Mary. Instead, he punched her hard, knocking her out cold. Then he turned on Hannah and threw her to the floor. He fell upon her, held her wrists tightly against the floor boards so she couldn't cut him again and put his scraggly-bearded face into her neck and worked his face down toward her bosom. Hannah screamed. He growled an obscenity and ordered her not to make another sound. He squeezed her right wrist so tightly that the dirk dropped free. He grabbed it and put it to her neck.

Hannah whimpered, prayed Logan would appear, and held her knees together as tightly as she could.

***

"JACK, YE CAN help Dougal bind up his wound, then hitch up the horses. I'll wake Mary and Hannah and bring 'em down."

He cared not a fig that they'd wasted coin on lodging, but he was concerned that they might be followed. It was best if they left now, before that bully McMillan replaced his injured pride with vengeance. There were definitely more McMillans than McKelveys in this part of Scotland, and though many seemed cowardly, he expected they'd increase their numbers before the sun was up.

He entered the inn and took the rickety stairs two at a time. He heard a woman's scream when he reached the top. There, on the left, was Hannah's door, wide open, candle light flickering and casting meaningless shadows on the floor. And beyond it another open door. His first thought was that perhaps Mary had screamed from a nightmare and Hannah had …

No! That was a man's deep growl he heard. He fumbled for his absent dirk, then drew out his axe and lunged for the first door, saw no one in his room and dashed on to Mary's room. A woman's form was on the bed, but there, on the floor, was his Hannah struggling to hold off a pig of a man.

Logan's reaction was quick and visceral. He sent the axe flying the ten feet it took to reach the man's left foot. Any other spot and he might have injured his wife, but his accuracy was as perfect as when he aimed at a tree. The man's response was to drop the dirk and howl like a cat. And between the high-pitched shrieks, he peppered his bawling with obscenities.

"Ye've chopped me foot off," he screeched.

Logan grabbed up his axe as well as his dirk. "Are ye all right, Hannah?" He pulled her to him with his free hand and they stood staring at the blood pouring from the wound. The foot was intact, but the ankle bone was undoubtedly broken.

Mary groaned and sat up.

"Get yerselves dressed. We're leaving." Logan pointed the dirk at the man. "Use the bed sheet to bind yer leg. What be yer name?"

The man sniveled and pulled at the corner of the bed. "I be Clyde McMillan and ye're wise to be leavin' or me brother'll slit yer throat fer me."

"Ye're lucky I dinnae aim fer yer head."

He felt Hannah clutch his other arm with both hands. He turned his attention to her.

Their departure was hurried but complete. They traveled several miles and most of the night until the horses were exhausted. They came to a bigger town and found safer lodging.

Chapter 16

L OGAN ARRIVED AT the run-down English inn, the one they had been staying at for the past day and a half while Dougal sought help for his injury and the women recovered from their ordeal. He had left earlier that morning to look for a church—unsuccessfully—but now upon his return, he found the door to his room was locked and Hannah was not answering his knock. He tried the door handle again in disbelief and felt a chill of fear run up his spine. Was nothing but trouble going to follow them on this journey?

Logan paced in the corridor, considering another way in. He hurried outside and spied their window, half-covered by ivy. With a deep breath, he grabbed hold of the window frame and pushed. Once he got it open wide enough, he climbed up and scrambled inside. His heart raced as he surveyed the room.

Empty.

But there was a second door, connecting it to Mary's room and there was Hannah, huddled in the corner with Mary, shaking, her face pale.

"Hannah," Logan cried out. He ran to her and pulled her into a tight embrace. She clung to him, trembling.

"It was awful, Logan," she said, her voice wavering. "An intruder came in the night and I fought him off with the dirk you left with me."

"I ken all that. It happened two nights ago." He glanced at Mary who shrugged her shoulders.

Logan closed his eyes, his heart aching for the fear she must have felt, and now to still think the terror was at hand. He held her close, stroking her hair and murmuring words of comfort.

"Shall I take ye back to our room?" he said, finally. Hannah snuggled into his arms and nodded her head.

He reached a hand out to Mary and said, "Are ye all right to stay alone?"

"'Twas a frightenin' experience, fer sure, but I'll be fine. The lass needs more time."

Logan thanked her for watching over Hannah while he was gone.

"Did ye find it? Was it where I told ye?"

He shook his head. "Nary a soul I passed had heard of that chapel."

"But Keir found it. He brought Eleanor the parchments ... his wedding gifts to her."

"Well, we lost a day of travel; we're nay as far as we should be. Perhaps on the morrow we'll find the church. But truly, any will do." He picked Hannah up and carried her in his arms like a baby. He looked at Mary as they got to the door. "We'll see ye in the morning, we'll get on the carriage and continue our journey. Are ye happy to be in England?"

"I should be," Mary mused, "but I'm a Scot now. I miss me lad, Colin ... and yer father."

Logan smiled back and went on into his room, laid Hannah on the bed, and sat on the edge.

Hannah peered up at him, her face still pale and her eyes still wide with fear. But she had courage, Logan thought. She had defended herself against the intruder, with his dirk, no less. He was so proud of her. He stroked her cheek, hoping her mind would return to the here and now.

He crawled into the bed with her, held his wife close, and whispered in her ear, "You're safe now. I will always keep you safe. I love you, Hannah."

***

HANNAH COULDN'T UNDERSTAND herself. Her sense of time had changed. For those awful few moments when she was on her back, the dusty floor boards hard against her head, time had slowed as every one of her senses engaged in the ordeal.

She still saw him. That reddish beard, those crazy blood-shot eyes, a nose with long and curly hairs to match his brows.

And smelled him. The scent of fermentation, cider or ale or maybe sour sweat.

And felt him still, despite being now wrapped in Logan's strong arms. The weight of the stranger upon her. His rough fingers on her wrists. The scratchy beard on her tender skin.

Two nights ago? What had happened to the time since? It had gone so fast, as if there was no time at all. Was she stuck in those few seconds? Doomed to think of nothing else?

"Hannah, ye're tremblin' still. What can I do to help ye, lass?" Logan's breath warmed her face as they lay together on the bed.

She didn't mean to cry, nor did she mean to laugh, but those were the sounds that came from her mouth, uncontrolled.

"Shh, shh," he pulled her closer, "I'll sing ye a soothin' cradle song. 'Twill settle ye."

He cleared his throat and started with a whisper of notes. His voice was low as he sang, "*Baloo baleerie,*" and a little louder as he reached the verse, "*Gang away peerie faeries,*" and then softened at "*Doon come the bonny angels.*" The tone was perfect, his baritone smooth and melodious.

Hannah's breaths shuddered at first and then found an even rhythm to match Logan's. The words she didn't understand were comforting just the same. She focused on Logan's face, the candle light enough to show not only his handsome features, but the love in his eyes.

"*Doon come the bonny angels, Tae oor ben noo.*"

She mouthed the words along with him as he sang the lullaby again.

Her body relaxed and when she closed her eyes it was no longer her attacker's face she saw, but Logan's. She felt his chest, his caressing hands. Smelled the leather of his belt, the wool of his kilt.

"*Sleep saft my baby,*
Sleep saft my baby,
Sleep saft my baby,
In oor ben noo."

***

LOGAN, MARY, DOUGAL, Jack, and Hannah—now nearly recovered—arrived at the English estate late the next day. A group of ruddy-cheeked boys in patched pants and worn shoes kicked a can along the cobblestone street of Feock, Cornwall, shouting at each other to pass the can their way. The carriage rolled to a stop in front of the manor. The front gardens and bushes had not been pruned of their winter-browned stems and blackened leaves. The stone path that led up to the front porch needed sweeping.

Jack dismounted. As soon as his feet hit the ground, a servant, barely out of his teens, slipped out the front door. He stood at attention, like a soldier, but his eyes followed the play of the town boys as they ran further down the street.

"We're here to see Nathaniel Pascoe," Jack said, drawing the lad's attention to him.

Before the servant could acknowledge that they were indeed at the right home, Logan climbed down from the driver's seat and opened the door to the carriage. "This is his daughter, Hannah Pascoe."

The lad was remarkably reserved and showed no surprise. "Yes, sir," he said. "She'll be the eighth Hannah Pascoe to arrive since he posted a reward in the Morning Chronicle." He looked Hannah up and down and then spotted Mary peering out the door. "You'll all need to wait outside. He'll only see the lady. Come, miss."

Hannah cocked her head at Logan who nodded back. "Go ahead, lass. 'Twill be fine."

The servant led her into the grand entrance hall and then into a smaller, darker sitting room. It smelled of cod liver oil, stale incense, and unwashed clothes, as if the place had been used as a hospital room for a lengthy amount of time. Neither space seemed familiar to Hannah. Her eyes eventually went to the back of the room, where a woman lay in a four-poster bed. A thin, sad-looking man sat at her bedside holding her hand. His face seemed pinched with worry; his eyes hollowed out by fatigue. He raised his head briefly to see the servant and Hannah. He waved them off.

"You're too late, I'm afraid. She hasn't stirred this last hour. If you've brought laudanum, it'll do her no good now."

"Sir," the servant bowed, "this is not the apothecary's daughter. She says she's … she's your daughter."

Hannah took a hesitant step forward so she could see the woman's face. It was thin and pale and deadly still, but her chest was moving faintly up and down with shallow breaths.

"Another one?" the man sighed. "Take her to Mildred and have her see if she bears the birthmark. I must remember to cancel the advertisement."

Hannah frowned, her thoughts instantly settling on the strawberry mark on the back of her thigh. She often forgot it was there as it was in a place too hard for her to see without a mirror, and besides, her legs were rarely bare. Eleanor was used to seeing it when they bathed but hadn't mentioned it in years. And only as recently as these last few days had anyone else seen all her skin. Logan had kissed her there and called the mark a second heart, one he'd treasure as much as her beating one. She smiled to herself as she followed the servant. She was so grateful to have Logan; if not for him she may not have recovered so well from the awful attack.

"Where are we going?" she asked as the servant took a long hall and then led her down a flight of stairs.

"To the kitchen, where Mildred, the cook, is. Mildred used to be the Pascoe children's nanny. There were four children she tended. Then typhoid fever took two and one died from dyptheria. Only Hannah lived through her illnesses … and then she was snatched away by baby stealers, though she was well beyond her baby years. Of course, if you're the real Hannah, you would know that." The young servant looked snidely at her. "Mildred is me mum's sister. She stayed on to be the cook once there was no hope of any more Pascoe heirs to look after."

They entered the kitchen and he hollered, "Auntie Millie!"

The phrase echoed in the depths of her memory, so familiar, as if she used to call for this person herself.

A woman as round as a copper tub was bent over a boiling pot of some delicious-smelling concoction. A chipped enamel teakettle and matching pot also sat simmering on the coal stove. The woman set down a wooden spoon and turned to her nephew. "What now, boy?" The raspy voice was unmistakable and conjured up for Hannah flashes of childhood events: burning a finger on a candle, falling out of bed, waking from a nightmare.

"Auntie Millie," Hannah croaked out, tears coming to her eyes. This was the person she remembered most. The woman who tended her scraped knees, kissed her forehead, tucked her in bed at night. This was the woman she mourned for in those early days when she mourned at all for the family she lost. She'd bonded so quickly to Eleanor that she let the old memories fade like morning dreams. "Auntie Millie, it's me, Hannah." She ran toward her and saw the doubt in the old woman's eyes. Hannah stopped, lifted her skirt, and brought the folds of the material up high enough to reveal the red spot—the birthmark Millie used to make up stories about every time she bathed her.

Millie's expression remained dubious. Hannah twisted to see for herself, afraid for an instant that perhaps Logan had kissed it away.

Then … "Hannah!" Mildred cried out. "'Tis you, indeed." She grabbed her in a bear hug and bounced her against her ample breast. "Oh, the master will be exultant. Oh, but no … the mistress." She released her and her brows knitted together in concern. "Come, let us hurry up to the sick bed. Your mother may not last the day." She tucked an arm through Hannah's and started pulling her forward before stopping so abruptly her wattled chin shook. She slapped a hand to her heart. "'Tis too much for these old legs. Tommy, take her up at once."

The servant, wide-eyed now and shocked at how much bare leg he had seen, took Hannah's hand and ran with her.

But this can't be happening, Hannah thought. She wanted to stay with Auntie Millie, hug her some more, cry on her shoulder, tell her how much she loved her and missed her, stare at her face and … and remember.

Tommy tugged her on the stairs and rushed her down the hall and through the entry, only slowing at the entrance to the former parlor now sick room.

"Sir … sir … Mildred says … 'tis your daughter … Hannah."

The man rose, bones creaking, and erased the distance between them with three long strides.

"Hannah? 'Tis really and truly you? Let me see your face." He tilted her chin up and studied her eyes, touched her nose, ran a finger along her jaw and smiled sadly. "Yes," he said, tears streaming down his cheeks, "I see it now. You've grown into a lovely young woman. Come. See your mother. She has but few breaths left. 'Twas her final wish to see you."

He called the sick woman Agnes, and the name aroused a memory. Hannah took the seat by the bed and reached for the dying woman's hand. "Mother?" The word felt strange on her lips. She tried it out again and squeezed the hand. Her father stood next to her and kept a warm hand on her shoulder. This was all too much to bear. Millie ... her mother ... this man she couldn't remember ... would her heart and head not burst in paroxysms of love and anguish and confusion?

The hand on her shoulder lifted and her father said, "Tommy, if there was anyone with Hannah, have them come in. Bring refreshments, too."

Logan and the others made polite introductions and bowed as they walked in, then all eyes remained on Agnes as they awkwardly stood around the sick bed. It was clear that her time on earth was running out.

Hannah was overwhelmed with emotion when she felt the slightest movement in her mother's hand and then her eyes opened. Agnes was too weak to speak, but she managed to turn her head slightly and look at her daughter. Her eyes filled with tears. She whispered something, and then, with one last look of love, she closed her eyes. And then her face went slack and her chest stopped its exhausted effort.

The room was silent for a few moments, until Tommy respectfully bowed and backed out of the room. Logan, Mary, Dougal, and Jack quietly stepped out too, leaving Hannah and her father alone with the body.

***

THREE DAYS LATER Hannah peered up from the desk in the parlor, where she had been engrossed in her mother's journals, to see her father watching her intently. He seemed to take up all the air in the room as he stood at the door frame his hand on the doorknob. His face was stern and his eyes far away. His looming presence had a strange effect on her— she felt a peaceful calm, yet her stomach was heavy with a strange dread that she couldn't place. These few gloomy days spent in this house, unfamiliar because it wasn't the one she was born in, had been full of momentary joy and eternal sadness. The four-poster bed had been removed after the wake.

"Hannah," he said, his voice deep and solemn.

"Yes, Father?" she answered, her voice soft and meek, her lips unused to these syllables.

He took a deep breath and let it out slowly.

"I have news," he said.

Hannah sat up straighter in her seat, her brow furrowing in confusion. What news could it be?

Her father approached the desk, his hands clasped behind his back.

"You have a distant relative by the name of Roger Tipsdale," he said.

Hannah furrowed her brow even more. She had never heard of this man before. She'd met so many relatives who attended the funeral, but none by that name.

"He is your mother's second cousin, a widower. He was at the funeral, but kept to himself though he saw you and wrote a most convincing letter to me, quite concerned with your grief." He cleared his throat and paused a moment. "He is heir to a great fortune. And, uh, he wants you to marry him."

The words hit Hannah like a shovelful of stable dirt. She stared at her father in shock, unable to comprehend what he was saying. Her mind went blank.

"He has offered to pay off my debts and make you the inheritor of his fortune," her father continued. "But only if you marry him."

Hannah's eyes widened in disbelief. Hadn't her father understood that she was handfasted to Logan? How could she marry a man she had never met even if she wasn't already betrothed? This Roger Tipsdale must be desperate if he was willing to make such an extravagant offer. Did he think her beautiful? He couldn't have seen her face behind the black veil.

"Father," she said slowly. "I'm handfasted to Logan."

Her father sighed and closed his eyes. "It doesn't matter," he said solemnly. "We ... I mean I ... I need the money. I'll lose this mansion and be forced to move out next week. This is the only way."

A wave of emotions washed over her. Disappointment, anger, sadness, confusion. She'd been stunned to learn there was great wealth in her family, stunned again to learn her father had lost it all, but what need had she for it? The McKelveys were well off, and she was a McKelvey now, wasn't she? This sudden marriage proposal was staggering. She couldn't possibly agree.

"Father," she swallowed twice, "I'm ... I'm no longer a virgin."

Her father acknowledged the struggle on her face. He reached out and patted her shoulder gently.

"He needn't know. Or we could say you were widowed ... I know this is a difficult decision," he said, "but it is one that must be made. Think on it, and let me know your answer in the morning."

With that, he turned and left, closing the door behind him.

Hannah stared at the door for a long time, her mind racing. She couldn't believe it.

With a heavy heart, she made her way to the guest room and collapsed onto the bed. She didn't move for a long time, her mind whirling with confused thoughts and emotions. What did she owe her father? And who was this Roger Tipsdale who would give his fortune to marry a woman he never met? Was he mentally afflicted or deformed or feeble minded?

***

LOGAN DIDN'T MIND sharing a room with his brother and Dougal. So much furniture had been sold off that the Pascoe estate seemed empty and far too large for only Nathaniel Pascoe, his servant Tommy, and the cook, Mildred. Mary and Hannah shared the only guest room that was adequately furnished. Logan's shared room was a storage room for old divans and cushioned chairs that had lost their filling, things that failed to sell. They'd helped move the four-poster bed back to the master suite where Nathaniel spent hours grieving. The Pascoes had been going through tough times for a while. Logan didn't snoop, but he was curious how the circumstances had become so dire.

He'd stayed at Hannah's side for the wake and the funeral, but spent whatever other free time during these days of mourning, riding Dougal's horse about the town, looking for a merchant who'd sell him the perfect gift for his new wife and secretly paying off some of Pascoe's debts.

He was pleased with Hannah's mental recovery from the attack. The hysteria she suffered had not returned. He did not like at all that they slept in different rooms, but their stay was limited; he expected to leave within the week.

The death of her mother was a horrendous blow, and yet it was not as upsetting to her, it appeared, as his own mother's passing had been for him. That was understandable, of course, but being reunited with her father was not going as expected. The man avoided Logan's attempts at conversation. Perhaps he needed to be alone to grieve; a hasty retreat might be best for all.

***

HANNAH SAT IN the servants' small dining nook next to the kitchen and commiserated with Mildred. Mildred had much to tell her, first of the year-long search for her after she was abducted—a king's ransom spent on sleuths and trackers and fortune tellers in an effort to find her. And then of her mother's multiple pregnancies thereafter—each child miscarried or still-born—and her father's growing debts resulting in the loss of maids, and footmen, and livery.

Hannah placed her hands on Mildred's plump palms. "I'm sorry for all their misfortune, but … I can't say I remember much about my father; I didn't even remember his name."

Mildred rolled her fingers over Hannah's. "I'm not surprised." She lowered her voice to a whisper. "He wouldn't have resumed the search for you if your mother hadn't gotten ill. It was her delirious rantings that spurred him to it, claiming she saw a vision of you as rich as a princess." She huffed under her breath. "Poor thing … but at least she got to see you before the end."

The two went still, staring at their tea cups and holding tight to the other's hands and to their memories.

Hannah broke the silence. "He wants me to marry a rich relative who'll get him out of debt. But, Auntie Millie, I can't. I've promised myself to Logan. We were handfasted."

"Oh … handfasting was banned here in England years ago, when I was a young girl. The marriage act stopped such clandestine unions."

"It's not uncommon in Scotland."

"Hmm. I don't know what to tell you, dear." She drew her hands back as if she heard something.

"Ah, I thought I'd find you here," Nathaniel Pascoe said upon coming down the back staircase. He clicked his fingers at Mildred and nodded at the teapot steaming on the stove. The cook grabbed the tea strainer and the pot and hurried to pour him a cup. He took her seat and neither thanked her for the tea nor apologized for intruding.

"I see that the three men who brought you are readying the horses and carriage. May I assume they are leaving? I rather like the lady who escorted you. She's most welcome to stay on as your maid. I'm sure Roger Tipsdale would approve." He took a sip and blinked at the steam.

"I'm sorry, Father," Hannah said, her voice breaking. "But I cannot do as you wish." She glanced over at Mildred who was refilling the strainer with fresh tea leaves, a fine, thin laugh line curving near her mouth. "I love Logan, and I cannot marry another man."

Her father's face darkened. "Logan? That blasted Scot? No, no, no." He set the cup down hard and spilled half the tea. He took a breath and calmed himself. "You are breaking my heart," he said with teeth clenched. "Very well," his voice was icy, "if that is your decision, then I must disown you. You are not my daughter. Another young girl pretending to be Hannah Pascoe will come to the door and I'll not look for a birthmark. Roger won't know the difference."

A heavy wave of sadness washed over her. She hadn't been expecting such callousness. If her father was this unreasonable, unfeeling, then she was glad she hadn't grown up in his care. Yet it still felt like a shocking blow, more so than seeing her mother die.

She stood and walked to Mildred, giving her a final embrace.

"Goodbye, Auntie Millie," she said, her voice trembling.

With that, she turned and rushed up the stairs, barely holding back the tears.

Logan was waiting outside, and when he saw her, he rushed to her side. He took her in his arms and held her tightly, letting her cry into his chest.

When finally she looked up at him, her eyes still full of tears, she said, "Let's go."

***

MARY STEPPED THROUGH the door and the musty-smelling church greeted her with a hush. The place seemed to hold its breath, waiting for something. She glanced around, taking in the dim glow of the candles noiselessly burning in the windows and the altar, the marble statues of saints, the sun streaming in through the stained-glass windows on one side. She glanced up at the wooden beams that stretched across the arched ceiling, like a loved one's outstretched arms.

It was then that she felt it, the warmth of fate that seemed to linger in the air, as if the church itself was embracing them all. She looked over to her companions, Dougal and Jack. Dougal was standing with his hands behind his back, his face softened in reverence, while Jack was looking around, eyes wide with wonder.

146

"This is the right church. Dougal, please tell Logan and Hannah to come in. Jack, you look for the priest."

Mary glanced around one more time before taking a deep breath and kneeling at the altar for a quick prayer.

Logan and Hannah came in slowly, he leading her softly forward up the aisle, she peering around and visibly shaking. Logan kept glancing at Hannah, his smile quivering, his eyes alight with hope and anticipation. And Hannah—Mary would remember to tell her daughter when she saw her—Hannah's expression, how she smiled at him, her heart obviously swelling with love. The poor dears had been through so much together, and Mary didn't know the half of it, but she did know that this moment would be the culmination of it all and the new beginning they needed.

"Are you ready?" Logan asked Hannah, his voice a whisper, though it carried in the high sanctuary.

"Yes," came Hannah's response, full of conviction. Mary was overwhelmingly happy for them.

Jack appeared with the priest, who walked to the front carrying a parchment, quill pen, and ink, and took his place to officiate.

He nodded at the couple, asked their names, copied them onto the parchment, and began the ceremony. Mary watched, her eyes misting over as they exchanged their vows. Her heart had been full to bursting the week before when she watched Eleanor wed Keir, and she felt the same hope and joy now as she witnessed another joining of lives.

***

LOGAN STATED EACH vow with confidence. On the inside he was gratefully thanking God that Hannah hadn't capitulated to her father's demand. He'd been outside the parlor when Nathaniel had pleaded for Hannah to wed the rich cousin. He considered stepping in and offering to pay all debts himself, but a hint of pride, and also curiosity, held him back. He needed to see for himself what she would decide. He'd been ready to leave without her if need be, though that would have broken his heart.

Now, here he was in as fine a cathedral as ever he'd seen, binding them closer, if that were possible, in a righteous union, blessed by a holy man.

He listened as Hannah spoke her vows, her eyes shining, her lips twitching to smile, her loveliness captivating him more in this moment than when they were handfasted.

And then, too soon, it was over. They signed the parchment and giggled. Jack and Dougal slapped him on the back while Mary kissed Hannah's cheeks.

Jack teased, "Ye need to kiss her, now, brother. I won't be satisfied 'til I see ye've made her squeal a wee bit."

***

HANNAH'S SPIRIT SOARED. She wouldn't let herself dwell a moment more, ever, on the two events of this journey that hurt her physically, mentally, and quite emotionally. Eventually she'd forget the attack and get over it, but her mother's death and her father's rejection would stay with her forever. But this moment—and all the moments she'd have with Logan—would raise her up. She'd long thought of herself as a nobody, but no longer. She'd found herself, not in this man, but with this man.

She lifted the pen from the parchment and handed it to the priest. She bowed her head and curtsied. She was surprised at how a thick piece of paper and some ink could make a difference in her mindset. *I belong to Logan and he belongs to me. Now no one can deny it.*

She breathed in deeply, memorizing everything: the faint scent of incense, the goosebumps on her arms, the Savior on the cross, the smile on Mary's face, the sound of two men snickering softly, and the touch of Logan as he drew her closer.

The kiss was full of promise, hope, and joy. When they pulled apart, everyone was smiling, even the priest.

Logan pulled her into another embrace and whispered in her ear. "I have a wedding gift for you. I'm going to pay off all your father's debts and, if you desire it, I'll send for Mildred."

"Oh Logan! I can't thank you enough." She pressed her lips against his again. Retreating footsteps barely echoed in the church as they were left alone.

A pure and genuine kiss beneath the cross was the perfect acknowledgement of their now blessed union.

"Ah, my little English maiden," Logan said as they walked out together, "you are so much more than that … and … you own my heart."

THE END

Please leave a review on Amazon. And pick up the next book in the series: THE HIGHLANDER'S HIDDEN CASTLE to find out who wins the Highland Games at Castle Caladh and who wins Jack's heart. Plus, there's news of Keir and Eleanor, Logan and Hannah, that will warm your heart.

Made in the USA
Middletown, DE
15 July 2025

10633655R00086